Over The Northern Range

The Empty Sword Saga, Volume 2

Jonathan Zobel

Published by Jonathan Zobel, 2023.

OVER THE NORTHERN RANGE

First edition. December 21, 2023.

Copyright © 2023 Jonathan Zobel.

ISBN: 979-8223338987

Written by Jonathan Zobel.

Table of Contents

To all my friends and family who have kept pushing me to be the best I can. Thank you for all your support!

Pronunciation Guide

Annalio. Ann-AL-Leo
Lulandal. Lu-lan-Dhal
Saralia. Sa-rail-lee-ah
Areiop. Are-EE-op
Atrian. A-tree-an
Karotos. Care-OH-toes.
Polyhorit. Poly-hor-it
Kearon. Key-air-on.
Ibexians. EYE-Bex-EE-ans.
Glarion. Glare-EE-on.
Flitnao. Flit-Nay-oh.
Monaria. Mow-nair-EE-ah.
Urano. OO-Rah-no.
Horiton. Hor-it-ton.

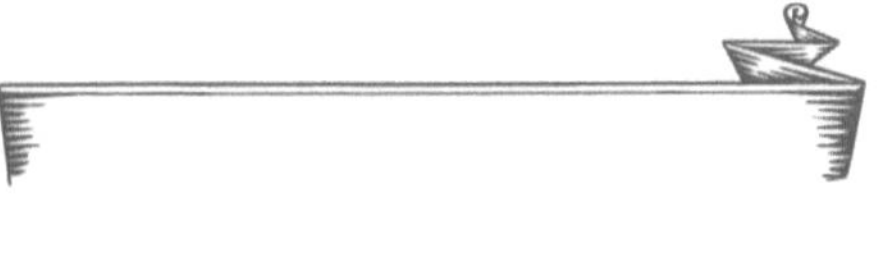

Chapter 1. Return.

Victoria fell back on her pillow and sighed. It had been a great summer so far. She had been spending time on her great-aunt Belinda's farm with her twin brother Stephen. So many things had happened, and she had trouble even believing some of them were real. She and her brother had gone into the forest behind their great aunt's house and somehow found their way into a whole other world full of fantastic creatures and they even got to be a part of a prophecy and help save it from an evil monster. But that was a week ago, now their friends Jack and Dani were spending the weekend with them on their way back from camp. She desperately wanted to tell Dani about their adventures, but she knew Dani would call her crazy and wouldn't believe her. Now Dani had just left their shared room and Victoria was alone, she rolled over and closed her eyes and she thought she could almost see some of their friends in that other world again.

"Tori."

The voice made Victoria sit up and look around only to see that there was nobody around.

"Tori!"

The voice called out again and Victoria saw a faint blue light come from under her pillow. She pulled it away and revealed a necklace with a golden pendant that she had hidden underneath it. It was given to her in that other world along with a beautiful sword and a flowing green dress she had worn on her first night in that fantasy world. It was one of the few bits of proof of their adventure she had, and she couldn't bear to keep it away from herself for too long. She gingerly picked it up and started to look at the engravings on it when it started to glow with a brilliant blue light. She gasped and dropped the pendant, and as soon as it left her hands the light vanished. She reached out and caught it before it could hit the ground and the light quickly returned.

Victoria watched in astonishment as particles of blue light poured from the pendant and moved into the center of her little bedroom. The light then formed into the shape of a young girl. The girl appeared to be around ten years old, with long hair in two braids that nearly went past her waist. Pointed, elf-like ears poked out through her hair and her cat-like eyes and six-fingered hands were clearly seen. She was wearing a long ornate dress with a belt holding a dagger around her middle. She looked at Victoria with a expression of surprise and worry.

"Tori? I... I didn't think this would actually work! But I can see you!" The girl exclaimed.

Victoria brushed some of her long black hair out of her face and rubbed her eyes.

"I can see you too! This can't be real!" She said as she looked at the figure in her room. The girl seemed to be one she had befriended in the other world. Victoria looked closer at the light formation and saw that it was indeed her friend Annalio, or as she preferred to be called, Annie.

"I wish I could be as excited as you. We need your help. There is something brewing outside of Lulandal's borders that we cannot handle on our own. We need you, Tori."

"I don't know if we even can come back!" Victoria said jumping off her bed and walking towards the apparition with her free hand outstretched. Annie reached out as well, and their hands almost seemed to meet but when they went to touch Victoria's passed through Annie's like a hologram.

"Please try. I do not know how much longer we can wait before something bad happens." Annie pleaded. Suddenly Annie turned towards the doorway and a look of fear swept over her as she let out a quick scream before she disappeared completely, and the light was sucked back into the pendant. Victoria stood in the middle of her room in shocked silence over what had just happened. But before she had a chance to process what had happened, she heard a voice from the doorway.

"What was that?"

Victoria spun around and saw the slightly over-five-foot figure of Dani standing in the doorway. She was wearing a pink nightgown and had paused mid-brush as she stood frozen in the doorway. Her face, which was very sleepy when Victoria watched her leave was now wide-eyed with excitement.

"Better question, who was that? And when do we leave?" Dani asked excitedly as she walked into the room and tossed her hairbrush into her bag.

"What do you mean?" Victoria asked.

"Don't play innocent with me. I know your dad is a tech genius, is that some new hologram device? Does someone need help?" Dani pleaded, her blue eyes sparkling with excitement.

"I wasn't sure how to tell you, but I guess I must now. You'd better sit down." Victoria said as she sat down on the edge of her bed and Dani quickly sat down next to her.

"You see over a week ago Steve and I heard about an old mansion that was supposedly out in the woods behind this house so we decided to go and exploring to see if we could find it."

"And you found something else instead?" Dani asked, twisting a lock of her shoulder-length blond hair in excitement.

"Something else indeed. We found the outside of a tunnel made out of trees and vines grown together, and after Steve made me fall through it, we decided to explore and see where it went. Soon we had realized we were in a different world altogether. A world with elves, centaurs, orcs, trolls, goblins, cat-ninjas, and birdmen. Of course, they weren't called that, and they were all different from what you've read in fantasy books but that's what they mostly looked like anyway."

"That sounds crazy! You're not pulling my leg, are you?"

"Not at all. I got this little pendant from that world after Steve, and I helped save it from a horrible creature called 'The Shadowed One' after many battles."

Victoria held out the pendant and Dani hesitantly took it and looked it over.

"It still doesn't seem real." Dani mused.

"I have trouble believing it myself sometimes." Victoria replied. "The girl you saw is named Annalio, but she prefers her friends to call her Annie. Steve and I saved her from the bad guys but sadly not before she was crippled by some monsters. But with the help of some new prosthetic legs, she is fine now. She gave me this pendant and said that she would be able to communicate through them, although she didn't know exactly how."

"So that girl wasn't some ghost or a hologram?"

"No, Annie must have figured out how to contact me, and now she needs help."

Victoria stood up from her bed and Dani followed suit.

"What do we do now?" Dani asked.

"I'm going to get Stephen up and see what he thinks."

"Are you going to tell Jack?"

"Only if I have to. I don't want to drag both of you into this."

The two girls walked silently down the hallway towards the boy's room and quietly knocked on the door. Getting no response, they opened it to find that the room was empty.

"Where are they?" Dani asked perplexed.

Victoria walked over to the window that looked out over the old farmyard and the barn. She took one look at the barn and turned around and hurried back to her room. Dani followed right behind her.

"Are they outside?" she asked.

"Nope, just in the barn, the lights were on when I looked." Victoria said before quickly grabbing some warmer clothes. "You may want to change; it can get cold outside at this time of night."

After hurriedly dressing, the girls snuck outside and towards the barn. As they got closer, they could hear Stephen and Jack talking loudly.

"I can't believe you found this in an abandoned house!" Jack exclaimed.

"I know right? It's awesome!" Stephen replied.

Victoria groaned softly to herself before pushing the door open and rushing inside. There she found her twin brother Stephen standing near one of the horse stalls and tall and lean frame of their friend Jack nearby swinging an ornate one-handed sword through the air. Both the boys looked up as Victoria and Dani entered the barn.

"Tell him the truth Steve." Victoria said. "Dani already knows. Annie needs our help"

Stephen's face went pale from surprise but quickly looked back at Jack who stared at him in shock.

"I earned this sword for saving another world!" Stephen said quickly to Jack before turning back to his sister and Dani. "How did you hear from Annie?"

"The pendants do actually work. She can talk to me through them. Now fill Jack in on the rest while I get my things ready. We should try to head out tonight."

Stephen quickly started telling a long-winded version of his adventure as Victoria entered another stall and found a large leather satchel and a sword in its sheath where she had hidden them under some hay.

"You wanted proof Dani? Here it is." Victoria said as she opened it to reveal a set of clothes an adventurer would wear in a fantasy book, a small pouch of other-worldly herbs, and a beautiful green dress. Dani looked on in amazement before Victoria put the satchel down and drew her own sword and checked its blade.

"You weren't kidding after all." Dani's voice trailed off as they heard someone else enter the barn. The girls hurried out to find the short but muscular frame of Stephen and Victoria's great aunt Belinda in the doorway.

"I know what you're up to." She said quietly. "You heard from your friends in Lulandal haven't you? I knew it was only a matter of time when I saw your pendant."

"How did you know they could do that?" Victoria asked.

Belinda responded by pulling a similar pendant from her pocket. "Because I have one too. These things are quite impressive, when two people with matching pendants touch them together under the light of the blue moonflower, their spirits are linked to the pendants and by using the same ancient power that the ancient artifacts use, one can talk to the other no matter the distance. Or at least that's what I was told anyways."

"So, I could try and... call Annie back?" Victoria asked.

"Or Groman?" Stephen chimed in.

"No, only those on the other side can contact you. I'm not certain why. But if your friend called out for help you should go in the morning. Those woods are dangerous after dark."

"But Annie said to go as soon as we could." Victoria pleaded.

"By now whatever was happening has happened and you will be too late anyway. Remember, their time is different from ours. Ready your things and get some sleep, then head out in the morning." Belinda said firmly before turning around and leaving the barn. The four teens looked at each other.

"Well Tori looks like we have some work to do." Stephen said as he put his sword back in its sheath.

"I can't wait!" Dani squealed excitedly.

"Wait! You're coming too?" Victoria asked.

"Of course. If it's as bad as it sounds, you'll need all the help you can get." Jack said rubbing a hand through his short brown hair.

"This place isn't some nice peaceful world. You're going to have to fight somewhere and last I heard, you don't have any sword fighting skills." Stephen said as he walked into the stall to return his sword.

"No, but I'm a decent shot with a bow." Dani countered.

"And my dad taught me some judo." Jack added.

"Look martial arts are nice but they really don't..." Stephen was cut off by Jack lunging forward, flipping him over his shoulder and onto the packed dirt. Stephen looked up at him in surprise.

"Alright! You're coming along! We'll find something for you to fight with when we get there!" Stephen said gasping for breath.

"Yes!" Dani shouted excitedly.

The next half hour the four of them quickly readied their things and then returned to the house where they did their best to get some sleep.

Chapter 2. Friends and Foes.

Stephen rolled over in his bed and stared at the ceiling. "What have I gotten myself into?" he thought to himself. He remembered what he and his sister had been through on their last visit to Lulandal. He did remember some of it fondly but other parts not so much. He shuddered as images of Victoria's and Annie's injuries came to mind. The sight of comrades fallen in battle, and the sheer terror he had experienced due to some of the creatures he had faced, what would they face now? What threat was so strong that Groman and his completed weapon couldn't handle it?

"Hey Steve, are you awake?" he heard Jack's voice coming from the mattress on the floor.

"No... yes." He replied.

"Are you excited about going back to the other world?"

"A little."

"A little? I thought you'd be sneaking out to go there right now!"

"Let's just say last time was rough. The battles we fought were rather bloody and I lost some friends over there."

"War is never a pleasant thing."

"But it was more than that! I watched comrades get injured and brutally killed, and I killed so many little monsters myself. I never thought much of it at the time but after getting beaten by one monster in particular, it all came back. And to top it all off... I nearly lost Tori. We were fighting the big bad himself... she got knocked away like a ragdoll... hit a large rock and... she was paralyzed... As you can see, she was healed by some unexpected help, but I don't want that to ever happen again."

Jack sat up and looked at Stephen with a knowing look on his face.

"Steve, I know it's been a while since we've been together, but I can tell you've changed. You sound just like my dad after he comes back from deployment. He doesn't like what he did, he doesn't like what he saw, but he does it to save other people. From what it sounds like if you and Tori weren't there that world would have been lost. Yes, you may have done some things you regret, but that doesn't mean you did wrong. And the fact you are willing to go again proves to me that you want to help, no matter the cost. That sounds like true heroism to me. As for making sure nobody else gets hurt I promise you that I will do everything in my power to keep the girls safe."

Stephen sighed and looked at his friend. "Whatever it takes?" he asked.

"Whatever it takes." Jack replied holding out his hand. Stephen reached out and shook it just as the sunrise broke over the treetops. The two young men looked at each other and smiled.

"Let's go save a world!" Jack said excitedly.

Dani sat at the breakfast table wolfing down a bowl of cereal and a plate of toast in her excitement about what she was about to do. She still found it hard to believe that in a few hours she could very well be in a different world, and she didn't know whether to be excited or nervous. Just then she heard footsteps coming down the stairs and saw Jack and Stephen entering the kitchen. Jack was in hiking gear while Stephen was dressed in a green tunic, brown leather vest, brown leather boots, and green trousers.

"You look like you just walked out of a fairytale!" she giggled.

"In a way I did. This is what I was wearing when Tori and I came back from our adventure." Stephen responded as he sat made himself a bowl of cereal and toast. Victoria then came down wearing a similar outfit to Stephen's only her boots had bits of metal armor plating covering them and her tunic and trousers were a dark blue. Her hair had been twisted into a single braid that fell down her back nearly to her waist.

"What do you think Dani?" She asked. "Do I look the part too?"

Dani nodded and quickly got up from the table just as Belinda entered the kitchen.

"I see you're all ready to go. Are you sure about this?" She asked quietly.

"Yes. Our friend needs our help." Stephen said firmly.

"And you two." She said gesturing to Jack and Dani. "Are you ready for whatever that world could throw at you?"

"Yes ma'am!" Jack said emphatically.

"I'm ready!" Dani chimed in.

"Are you sure?" Stephen asked. "I have no guarantee this will be an easy journey."

Jack hesitated but then replied. "I know I can handle whatever this world sends my way."

Stephen glanced at Jack and noted he looked a little nervous, but Belinda broke his train of thought with a question.

"Do you have weapons for them to use? You'll probably need them before you meet up with your friends." Belinda asked.

"Dani can use my dagger if she needs it. My sword should be enough for me." Stephen replied.

"What about me?" Jack asked before noticing Belinda was sizing up his six-foot frame.

"You seem like a strong young man. Here," she said reaching around the corner and producing a large, black, two-handed sword with its belt and sheath. "You can probably use this fairly well."

Jack slowly reached out and took the large weapon.

"Aren't you coming too Aunt Belinda?" Victoria asked. Belinda sighed and leaned against the doorframe.

"There is nothing left for me there." She said quietly.

"Why do you say that?" Stephen asked.

"You know how your pendant was linked to your friend's?" She asked.

Stephen and Victoria both nodded. Belinda then pulled out a silver pendant much like Victoria's and looked at it.

"Mine was linked to the one you know as The Golden One. There came a day that I somehow knew my closest friend had passed, and when you returned and confirmed my suspicions it only strengthened my resolve to not return. However, I will not keep you from going so long as you know what you are getting into. And please make sure to stay safe. I don't want to have to be the one to explain your disappearance to your parents."

With that, Belinda hugged all of them and went back upstairs. The four teens quietly left the house and walked down to the barn where Stephen and Victoria's weapons were waiting. Stephen and Victoria strapped their swords to their belts while Dani hooked Stephen's twelve-inch dagger on her jean's belt loop. Jack strapped the two-handed sword to his back while Victoria gathered up the healing herbs in the satchel and then they were ready to head out.

Just as they neared the tree line Victoria looked back at the house and spotted Belinda watching them from an upper story window. She and her friends turned around and waved before disappearing into the thick forest.

For short Dani it was rather easy going as she could squeeze under most of the branches and undergrowth, for her friends however, it was different.

"Ouch! Watch that branch!" Jack cried as he walked into a tree limb.

"Which one?" Dani teased as she walked under the same branch with ease.

Jack grumbled while Victoria quietly laughed. After nearly an hour of pushing through the woods they came upon a small clearing where they stopped for a moment.

"I'm going to see if I can spot the trail from here." Victoria said before quickly climbing a tree.

"I doubt you could see anything in this mess." Jack muttered.

"Well how about that?!" Victoria called down. "I can see it!"

Stephen and Dani smirked at Jack who rolled his eyes.

"Where is it?" Stephen called out.

"About half a mile to our left! It looks different though." Victoria said as she climbed down.

"Well then let's keep moving. I'll try and make an easier path." Stephen said as he unsheathed his sword and began to cut his way through the undergrowth. The others followed at a safe distance. After a while of cutting Stephen stopped and looked ahead.

"Hey you're right! I can see the top of the wooden tunnel!" he shouted before sheathing his sword and breaking into a run. "It's right over..." He was cut off as he disappeared from view.

Victoria heard a short shout from her brother followed by a loud splat. The trio hurried over to find Stephen had fallen on his hands and knees into a muddy creek bed.

"Don't just stand there! Help me out!" Stephen called out over their laughter.

Soon Stephen had been freed and the foursome crossed the shallow creek bed and were now standing at the base of what looked like an archway made out of trees and vines.

"This might be a different part of the tunnel than the one we found." Stephen said as he wiped the mud off his hands onto a nearby tree.

"Yeah you cut a hole in the last one. Looks like we'll have to do it again." Victoria agreed.

The twins drew their swords and quickly hacked a hole in the wooded wall. As soon as they stepped away Dani raced past them and ducked inside the tunnel.

"Wow! Its bigger than I thought!" She called out of the tunnel. "Must be at least nine feet tall and ten feet wide in here!" she pulled a sketchbook out of her backpack and started to draw the tunnel's interior.

"Do you always have that thing with you?" Jack asked as he pushed his way into the tunnel.

"I never leave home without it. Besides, I want to chronicle our adventure." Dani replied.

"This is definitely a different part of the tunnel." Stephen said as the rest of the group squeezed inside. Once they were together again Jack squatted down and studied the tunnel floor.

"Horse prints? And does that footprint have six toes?" he said puzzled.

"That would be Trodontian and Kittrian tracks." Stephen replied. "The trodontians are basically centaurs, and the kittrians are kinda like elves but they have twelve fingers and toes. Oh, and they can change the color of their skin and clothes to turn invisible too!"

Jack gave Stephen a quizzical look before a chirping noise was heard above them.

"You have got to be kidding me! Not these guys again!" Stephen groaned as he couched low to the ground behind Victoria. Victoria giggled and Jack and Dani looked on in amazement as a bright red blur flew past their heads and settled on Stephen's shoulder, purring contentedly. Stephen stood up and faced his sister. Jack and Dani looked at Stephen's new friend and saw that it was a bright red lizard with six legs and large fleshy wings that folded up along its body. It seemed to smile as it rubbed its face against Stephen's, purring all the while.

"Why is it always me?" He whined as Victoria gently lifted the lizard's tail and found a small piece of rolled up paper tied to it. She pulled the paper off and read its message.

Steve and Tori.

I hope my little flyer finds you soon. We need your help in Areiop as soon as you can find us.

Annalio.

"Well, I would say we are on the right track." Victoria said as she pocketed the note.

"I just hope we're close to Areiop. It was a good day's walk last time." Stephen said as the lizard took off once more and flew down the tunnel ahead of them.

"Follow that lizard!" Victoria shouted as they hurried along the wooded tunnel at a brisk pace. Soon they came around a bend and saw a large clearing and a wooden wall ahead of them.

"Hey! That's Areiop!" Victoria shouted as the group slowed their pace to a walk.

"Wait, do you hear that?" Jack said looking around.

The rest of the group stopped and listened. Soon strange screeching and growls were heard all around them.

"We've got company!" Dani shouted.

"Get ready!" Stephen called out. The group drew their blades and the two men got in front of the girls.

"Protect the ladies at all costs!" Jack shouted nervously. He gripped his large sword so tightly his knuckles turned white, and he gritted his teeth awaiting whatever was about to come out of the woods.

"I can handle myself thank you." Victoria retorted as she pushed her way between the two men.

Suddenly dozens of small creatures began to swarm out of the woods in between them and the city. They were between two to three feet high, had glowing red eyes, rough grey skin, long sharp claws on their hands and feet, and they were all rushing towards the group.

"Gritters!" Stephen called out.

Soon it was just chaos as all of them were desperately fighting and trying to keep from being overwhelmed by the small creatures.

"I can't hold them back forever!" Jack shouted as he swung his sword in a wide arc cutting through three gritters at once.

"Hold on! Help is coming!" A voice shouted from behind them.

Dani turned to look to see who had spoken when she saw three gritters turn around and jump at what seemed to be thin air but the gritters landed on something she couldn't spot and whatever they were on started screaming like a young girl.

"Annie!" Victoria shouted as she quickly turned around and raced towards the gritters who were flying around. The two men held the monsters back as the two ladies rushed to the unseen person's aid.

"Tori! Help!" the invisible figure shouted as it raced towards Victoria and Dani the three gritters still holding on tightly, seemingly flying or being dragged by thin air. With three quick strokes the offending gritters were lying dead on the ground and to Dani's surprise, a young girl materialized near her. She was unlike anyone Dani had ever seen. She was a few inches taller than Dani herself and wearing a green dress and a brown cloak, she had pale green skin, bright green eyes with narrow, cat-like pupils, long white hair that was in two braids down her back, pointed ears, and six fingers on each hand. Before Dani could really process what, she was looking at, more gritters began to emerge from the woods. Victoria raised her sword and Annie pulled out a twelve-inch dagger.

"There's no end to these guys!" Jack shouted over the noise of the gritters.

"Help is coming!" Annie shouted as she slashed at a gritter who had gotten too close for liking.

Jack looked at the large mass of gritters. He knew he couldn't keep going forever, his breath seemed to get shorter by the second. Just as he was about to reach for his inhaler he had hidden in his pocket, several arrows sped past him and struck down three gritters that had just emerged from the woods. That's when he heard someone approaching on horseback. He looked over and saw that there was indeed someone coming but he had never seen anyone like them before. The person looked to be nearly nineteen years old, she had long blond hair in a single braid down her back, a muscular body, and was wearing a grey deerskin shirt. But what really caught his attention was that from the waist down she had the lower body of a horse. The horse half was light brown, and the tail matched her hair and was also in a braid. She had a longbow and quiver strapped to her back and she was busy cutting her way through the monsters with twin, curved scimitars.

"Saralia!" Victoria shouted. "It's good to see you!"

"Save the talk until after the fight!" The strange girl shouted as she continued her charge.

Just then all the combatants seemed to pause as a deafening roar that seemed to shake the trees was heard. A large log the size of a small car came flying through the remaining gritters and sent them scattering away. Then an enormous ten-foot-tall creature, dressed in dark green garb burst through the trees and started swinging a tree like a huge club, sweeping the gritters away like mere insects.

"Tiny!" Stephen shouted.

Hearing Stephen's shout the massive creature turned to face him, and its rough, grey face broke into a wide grin revealing rows of sharp teeth. Its red eyes seemed to glow in the daylight as it started to push through the dozens of gritters that remained.

"Little soldier! Little girl! Tiny very happy to see you!" Its loud voice boomed as it reached Stephen and Victoria and nearly crushed them in a bear hug.

"I'm happy to see you too!" Victoria wheezed as she began to run out of air. "Could you let me go? I can't breathe!"

"Tiny sorry!" Tiny said as he released the twins from his embrace.

Just then Saralia galloped over and skidded to a stop.

"That was the last of them. I got here just in time." She remarked before looking over at Jack and Dani who were staring at her and Tiny. "I see you brought friends."

"I'm Jack Briggs and this is my good friend Dani Wyng." Jack said.

"Did you forget to tell them about us?" Saralia asked.

"We only just found out about this world last night." Dani said as she turned away sheepishly. She felt bad for staring at these strange people, but she had never seen anyone like them before.

"Last night?" Annie asked. "I talked to you two days ago! I would have tried to contact you again, but I lost my pendant."

"Well, we're here now." Stephen said.

"What's going on? And where's Groman?" Victoria asked.

"That is what I would have told you if I had my pendant." Annie said looking at the humans as her eyes welled up with tears. "Groman has been kidnapped."

Chapter 3. Armed and Ready.

"What do you mean he's been kidnapped?" Victoria asked.

"We had been getting reports of some strange activity on the northern range, so Groman and I came to Areiop to help defend the city if it was to be attacked. The evening of the same day I tried calling to you with the pendant, we were attacked by some stealth fighters. I managed to hide but I lost my pendant in the scuffle. After I heard it was safe to come out, I was told that Groman had been carried off by those things." Annie replied nearly in tears.

"What did they look like?" Stephen asked.

"They looked a lot like the Blackmians, but yet they were different. Their faces were round instead of pointed and their eyes were large, they seemed to see well in the dark, and their screams..." Annie shuddered. "Were incredibly terrifying."

Victoria put a hand on Annie's shoulder.

"Don't worry. We'll get him back." She said firmly. "We just need to gather an army together and."

"I am afraid that will not be possible." Saralia said cutting Victoria off. "It is the gritter's nesting season. Once every year they try to find new places to form a nest for their queens. There are raids like this on nearly every city on a daily basis. Mother and Trakken are busy defending Prarait, Vulant is dealing with the black marketeers and gritters in Altimi, and Ripper is trying to help rebuild his own town. I was on my way over to do some trading when I got a message from

Annie saying she managed to contact you and that you were on your way."

"So, it's just us then?" Jack asked.

"I am coming too." Saralia said firmly.

"Me too. I am going to do whatever it takes to get my brother back." Annie responded.

"Tiny help little people." Tiny said with a big smile.

"Alright then. Jack, you and Dani can stay here in Areiop and..."

"Stay put?" Dani interrupted Stephen.

"I don't think so. We're coming too." Jack retorted.

"I guess we'd better get you the proper gear." Stephen said.

"I can help with that." Annie said.

Soon the four humans and their companions were inside the city of Areiop at the home of the village elder. Stephen, Victoria, and Annie were waiting in the main room while Jack and Dani were in adjoining rooms. Saralia had gone to the smithy to fetch proper weapons for the newcomers. Soon Jack exited the room in an outfit similar to Stephen's, only he was in a brown tunic and trousers.

"I gotta say this is pretty comfortable." Jack remarked.

"They don't make them like that in our world." Stephen added.

"I'll say." Dani said as she came out into the main room. She was wearing a long dark green dress with a tan vest.

"Are you sure you want to go with that?" Victoria asked.

"Positive. I'll never get another chance like this again, so I want to go all out!" Dani replied giving the dress a little twirl.

"I think you look great!" Annie giggled.

"I guess that settles it." Victoria said. Just then they heard a voice from outside.

"By The One Above are you going to come outside to choose your weapons, or should I just carry them back?" Saralia shouted.

The five of them went outside to where Saralia had set up a table that was now covered in all kinds of different weapons.

"I suggest you find out what suits you best now before we leave. I do not think you will find any better weapons in the mountains or whatever lies beyond them." Saralia said.

Stephen, Jack, and Dani hurried over to the table and began to look over the swords, shields, daggers, spears, clubs, maces, and everything else that the smithy had brought for them while Victoria stood by and sighed.

"I wish I had my tekko kagi claws back." Victoria said.

"Is that what they were called?" Saralia asked.

"Yes. I'd use them again in a heartbeat, but they were shattered in the fight against the shadowed one."

"Well then I guess you will want these." Saralia reached into one of the saddlebags that she had strapped to her horse flanks and pulled out a pair of strange looking weapons. They were two metal claws mounted to two metal bars that were fitted with leather straps which would fasten to the user's wrists and forearms. The claws extended about ten inches from the user's hands.

"Trakken said that he wished he could be here to help, but he figured this would do the job for him. When he heard of Annie contacting you he had these ready by the next day and told me I was to bring them to Areiop in hopes you would be there." Saralia said with a smile before handing the weapons and their holsters to Victoria. Victoria eagerly took them and tried them on.

"I feel like I used them only yesterday." She said with a grin.

"It was over a week ago." Stephen shot back as he picked up a large shield and strapped it to his back.

"Over a month for us." Annie said as she strapped her elegant dagger to her side.

"Time does really go differently for the two worlds." Jack said as he eyed a large crossbow.

Dani picked up a beautiful composite bow and pulled back on the string.

"You have a good eye. I made a bow just like it when I was a little child. It does take some effort pull it like larger bows but it is much smaller and easier to manage." Saralia said as she walked over to Dani.

"I took some archery classes when I was at a camp a few weeks ago. Since I don't really know how to fight with a sword, I guess this is my next best option." Dani replied.

"Are you good with a bow?"

"I wasn't too bad a shot with one at camp."

Saralia handed Dani an arrow and pointed at a small squirrel-like creature on the roof of a nearby house.

"If you can hit that nut-snatcher I will personally keep you supplied with all the arrows I can make."

Dani took a deep breath and put the arrow on the string. She closed one eye and aimed for the little creature that seemed to stop and watch her. She released the arrow, and it trimmed the fur off the tip of its bushy tail. The creature shook one of its four front legs making some sort of chattering noise almost like it was shouting at Dani before racing away.

"Excellent shot." Saralia remarked before handing Dani a quiver full of arrows. Dani nodded and quickly strapped the bow and quiver to her back. She also picked up an ornate dagger and attached its sheath to her belt.

Jack placed a crossbow on his back as well as a quiver of bolts for it. He also picked up a one-handed sword and tied it to his belt.

Once the adventurers were ready, Tiny arrived with a large bundle. He promptly dropped it on the table and stepped back smiling.

"Warm clothes for mountain walking." He said proudly.

The group walked over and found enough warm cloaks, hats, boots, and gloves for everyone.

Dani saw Annie grab a hooded cloak and gloves while longingly looking at a pair of boots. Dani took the boots and held them out to Annie before noticing Victoria staring at her in surprise.

"Dani she..." Victoria started to say but Annie held up her hand and stopped her.

"It is alright. I do not need those, thank you anyway Dani."

"What do you mean? You'll probably get frostbite if you don't wear them." Jack said before Stephen silenced him with a stare.

"Not a concern for me." Annie said before sitting on a nearby barrel. She reached down under her dress and pulled at something, the group heard a loud click and then Annie pulled out a metal prosthetic right leg with an intricately designed ankle joint. She set it down and quickly pulled off her prosthetic left leg. "I lost my lower legs due to the combined efforts of a traitorous elder, a monster, and myself trying to escape capture. I do not have to worry about that sort of thing anymore." She said with a weak smile.

Dani blushed and turned away.

"Sorry. I forgot; Victoria only told me last night." Dani said quietly. Annie reattached her metal limbs and walked over to her.

"It is alright. I try not to let it bother me too much." Annie said reassuringly.

Then Saralia stepped forward and stomped the ground with a front hoof.

"Does everybody have everything they need?" She asked. The rest of the group nodded. "We do not know what lies beyond the northern mountains. I suggest you make sure you are ready for whatever we may encounter on our journey. Tiny and I can carry anything you cannot."

The group double-checked their packs and gear and gave whatever they could not carry to the stronger members of the group. When they were done Saralia spoke up again.

"If we are all ready, I think we should head north. We should be able to reach the base of the mountains by dusk if we start now. Also, I would not suggest traveling at anything more than a normal pace. Hurrying only causes one to lose hope faster and I do not intend to gallop all day and night again." Saralia said.

The group nodded and they began to walk towards the gate where they were met by an older kittrian man.

"Elder Gilder. Have you come to see us off?" Annie asked the old man.

"Yes, little one. May The One Above keep you safe and grant you a safe return." The elder replied solemnly. Stephen, Victoria, Annie, and Saralia nodded quietly before they walked through the gate and back into the forest. As the walls disappeared from view Tiny turned around and waved back at the city walls.

"Bye home!" He said happily before turning back towards the group.

The party began the slow journey northwards through the thick woods pausing every now and then to disentangle someone, usually Saralia or Tiny, from a bush or vine. Suddenly Jack held up a closed fist and crouched down. The rest of the humans and Annie quickly followed suit.

"Do you hear that?" Jack asked.

"That screeching noise?" Saralia replied.

"Yeah. Isn't that more of those gritters?"

"It sounds like there are a few nearby, yes." Saralia said peering intently into the woods.

"Only a few? We can take them." Dani said drawing her bow and laying an arrow on the string.

"That will not be necessary." Annie replied. "Tiny and I can deal with them. Right Tiny?"

Tiny smiled and nodded before tilting his head back and letting loose a deafening roar that shook the surrounding trees. As soon as Tiny stopped, they could hear the sounds of the gritters scurrying away.

"They are probably survivors from that raid we stopped earlier. I like to walk through these woods and Tiny is my bodyguard when Groman is busy. One roar from him sends most of those pests running." Annie said with a grin.

"So, Tiny you've been living in Areiop for a while now?" Stephen asked as they resumed their journey.

"Tiny get here two days after little soldier and little girl leave. Tiny been big help working at new home since." Tiny replied with a wide smile.

"He is a great helper. We could not have finished the new great hall without his hard work." Annie said.

"I'm glad to see you doing well here. I can't thank you enough for what you did for me after our first meeting." Victoria said. Tiny's smile brightened and he gently picked Victoria up and set her on his shoulder.

"Tiny like helping where Tiny can. If Tiny can help, Tiny will. Tiny sorry for what shadowed one did to little girl, Tiny want to help fix little girl so Tiny did. Tiny now want to help find sword man and make pretty girl happy again." Tiny said quietly before setting Victoria down on the ground again.

After an hour of pushing through the woods they came to the open plains to the north, and they could see the peaks of the northern range towering over them to the north.

"Welcome to the Icy Prairie. Home of few friendly creatures and fewer people. There is a farm at the base of the mountains where we can stay the night." Saralia said. "From there it is a steep climb up those mountains and whatever is waiting for us there."

"Are you sure about climbing those mountains Sara?" Victoria asked.

"I have heard legends about a trail that goes to the top, but I have not seen it myself. In any case I brought my spiked ice shoes with me, so I will be able to climb just as good, if not better, then most of you." Saralia replied with a wink.

The party moved on across the open fields. Stephen noticed that it was beginning to get colder as they continued. He walked over to Saralia's saddlebags and pulled out his cloak and slipped it on. He looked around and noticed Annie and Dani were shivering together as they walked, and he quickly tossed them their cloaks. Annie nodded her thanks, but Dani picked up her pace and went over to Stephen.

"Steve, Annie hasn't said anything, but I can see she is falling behind. I think her legs are beginning to hurt." Dani whispered.

"Well, we can't have that, now can we?" Stephen said quietly. He fell back behind Tiny and said something to him quietly. Tiny smiled and with one motion scooped Annie up in his big hand and cradled her like a baby.

"Tiny? What are you doing? I can walk." Annie said.

"Tiny want to help. Tiny carry pretty girl." Tiny replied simply.

"Well, if you insist." Annie said hiding a look of relief on her face.

After another two hours of walking the group spotted some smoke coming from a few wooden and stone buildings in the distance.

"There it is Frostbite farm." Saralia said.

"Is there normally that much smoke coming from it?" Stephen asked.

Saralia looked into the distance and then gasped, "The One Above! The farm is on fire!" Saralia grabbed Jack and Stephen who were closest to her and quickly placed them on her horse half. Tiny scooped up Victoria and Dani and the group broke into a run.

Chapter 4. Higher and higher.

Despite her two riders Saralia quickly began to outpace Tiny as they rushed towards the pillar of smoke that was rising in the distance. Jack and Stephen held on tightly as the farm drew ever close. But as they neared, they heard a loud screech and before Stephen had a chance to react, he was snatched up off Saralia's back and into the air being carried higher and higher.

Victoria saw it all from her position in Tiny's arms. A greyish black blur rocketed down from the sky and within moments had picked up Stephen and was now carrying him screaming into the air. Dani tried to get an arrow on the string, but Victoria held her back.

"Don't shoot. That's a friend of Stephen's. Likely just having some fun at his expense." She said with a quick laugh.

That's when they noticed an acrid smell coming from the farm. Tiny's face wrinkled at the stench, and he slowed his pace.

"Why are you slowing down?" Dani shouted. "We need to help that farm!"

"Farm not on fire." Tiny said panting. "Tiny know smell. Smell is burning gritter. Not burning wood."

While Tiny and the girls were having this revelation, Stephen was still screaming his lungs out as he watched the ground fall away from him.

"Hello to you too!" A cold voice shouted over the wind in Stephen's ears.

"Peri?" he asked in surprise.

"By The One Above, how many times do I have to tell you? My name is Peregrine. Do not make me drop you."

"Did you start that fire? We were trying to help that farmer!"

"No. The farmer started it."

"Why?"

"To get rid of the dead gritters I killed."

"What?"

"The farmer hired me to keep the gritters away from his farm. Did your friends neglect to tell you it was nesting season?"

Stephen watched as they leveled off and he could see the farm more clearly. There was a large pile of burning gritters just outside the farm and he could just barely see Saralia and Jack talking to what he assumed to be the farmer.

"So, you saw us coming and wanted to have some fun?" Stephen said as he looked up at Peregrine's smiling face.

"Correct. Now I can go higher, or you can return to solid ground."

"I'd rather be back on the ground as soon as possible thanks." Stephen said before quickly realizing his mistake. Peregrine simply grinned and Stephen felt his stomach go into his throat as she began a steep dive towards the ground. Peregrine's wings bent inwards as she entered a falcon dive and the two of them rocketed towards the ground. Stephen thought he may be screaming again but he couldn't hear anything over the noise of the air rushing past his face. He closed his eyes and waited for the end.

On the ground, Tiny and the girls had finally joined Saralia and Jack by the mound of burning gritters.

"Quite a mess you got here sir." Victoria said as she leapt to the ground from Tiny's arms. "Did you and Peregrine kill all these yourselves?"

The old kittrian farmer looked at the newcomers with a icy stare. "We had some help." He gestured to a figure emerging from a nearby barn with a pile of more gritters in its arms. It was a nearly nine-foot-tall unkarian, when it looked over and saw the party it glared at them before tossing the dead gritters on the burning heap and turning away. Dani heard a low growl come from Tiny, but she didn't think much of it as she watched Saralia walk over to the farmer.

"So Atrian. Could we spend the night here before continuing our journey over the mountains tomorrow?" Saralia asked. Atrian looked at her with a look of annoyance.

"I do not have much room for more people. Much less for free. Did you bring anything worthwhile for trading?" Atrian said.

"No, I thought you would be willing to be let us stay out of the kindness of your own heart. This girl's brother was kidnapped, and we are trying to rescue him as soon as..." She was cut off by Stephen's scream overhead as he and Peregrine rocketed past before zooming back into the sky. Victoria and Dani laughed a little before turning back to the conversation.

"Look. I am a busy man and I do not have time to let a bunch of people just stay at my farm. If you are going to spend the night, you will have to earn your keep by doing a few jobs for me. My unkarian is still cleaning up the mess from the raid earlier and could use some help." Atrian said.

Just then Peregrine and Stephen swooped in and landed. As soon as Stephen's feet touched the earth, he bent down to kiss it only to get a mouthful of gritter blood and mud. He retched onto the ground before standing up while looking at the group and glaring at Peregrine who was still grinning. Dani and Jack couldn't help but stare at Stephen's captor. She was just barely shorter than Jack and had a pointed, bird-like face with long black hair. She had a pair of massive grey wings with black edges on her back, a grey and black tail, and her arms and legs were shaped like a bird's, covered in yellow scales and tipped with sharp black talons. Her knees bent backwards like a bird's as well. Her body was covered in matching grey and black feathers, and she was wearing a brown tunic and breeches that ended at her backwards bending knees. A pair of daggers hung at her belt and a longbow and quiver of arrows hung on her back. Jack and Dani's train of thought was broken by Saralia clearing her throat.

"If you insist." Saralia said.

"I do. Now you could go see if those pests left my grain wagon alone in the field and bring it back here. You young ladies can go help my wife prepare dinner in the house. You two men and the big unkarian can help clean up the rest of the gritters and then move some hay around in the barn for your beds. I do not have room in the house for you all."

The group nodded and soon set about their tasks. Victoria, Dani, and Annie went into the house where the found the farmer's wife hard at work in the kitchen.

"You must be some of the visitors Atrian was talking to outside." She said with a smile that revealed many missing teeth.

"That's us." Dani said.

"If you are here to help me there is much to do. Especially if that other unkarian is hungry. He is the biggest one I have ever seen. No doubt a big appetite."

"He does tend to eat a lot." Annie said with a smile.

Soon the girls were doing their best to keep up with the farmer's wife as they prepared a hearty meal of stew and roasted vegetables. As they were hard at work Atrian walked into the kitchen.

"How soon will my food be ready?" He asked roughly.

"A few minutes more. The karotos need time to cook properly." Annie said cheerfully while stirring a cauldron of stew.

"Well get it to me as soon as they are ready. Fighting gritters gives me a large appetite."

Just then the jar of spices Dani was carrying slipped from her hands and shattered on the floor. The farmer exploded with anger.

"Watch what you are doing you clumsy fool! Those spices cost a fortune in the Areiop market!" He shouted. Dani got down on her knees and tried to scoop some of the salvageable spices into a pouch when the farmer slapper her hand away.

"It is too late for that! Once they are on the ground the spices are ruined! Just clean it up and get another jar from the cellar!" he said before roughly pulling Dani to her feet. Victoria slowly reached for her weapons but felt a hand on her wrist. She looked over to see Annie shaking her head.

"I'm sorry sir it won't happen again." Dani said quietly.

"It had better not." Atrian growled before leaving the room with his wife following close behind him.

Dani sank to her knees and started shaking. Victoria quickly hurried over and knelt down beside her.

"Are you ok?" Victoria asked.

"Just give me minute." Dani replied in a whimper.

"Are you sure?"

"Yeah." Dani said as she shakily stood up. "I'm used to a lot worse than that. Just brought back old memories is all."

"If you say so."

"I will go and help you get another jar from the cellar Dani." Annie said. "I know what he is looking for."

The two girls entered the dark cellar through a trap door leading to a steep staircase lighted by a solitary lantern.

"Are you sure you are alright?" Annie asked when they were far enough away from the opening.

"Yes. That wasn't my first time being harassed like that." Dani replied quietly.

"Oh, I am sorry. Did something happen back in your world?"

"I'd rather not talk about it."

"Alright. But if you ever need to talk to someone, try Tiny. He is a great listener and smarter than he sounds."

Dani chuckled. "I can see that already."

The girls found the new jar of spices and returned to the kitchen to find Victoria and the farmer's wife starting to ladle the stew into two wooden bowls.

"You are just in time. Put some of that into Atrian's bowl and I will take it up to him." She said.

Annie hurried over and put a pinch of spice into each bowl while Dani stood back and watched.

"You girls can carry that cauldron over to the barn and start serving the others. I will be out there shortly with some bread." The farmer's wife said before leaving the room.

"We should hurry, I am sure everyone else is hungry too." Annie said as she grabbed a stack of bowls and spoons.

Victoria and Dani carried the cauldron between them to the barn while Annie led the way. When they arrived, it was nearly dark. They found Jack and Stephen sitting on a pile of freshly strewn reddish hay talking to Peregrine while Saralia, who was all muddy from the fields, stood nearby trying to stomp some mud off her hooves.

"Dinner is served!" Dani shouted as they entered the barn. Everyone quickly gathered around the cauldron and Victoria started ladling the still warm stew into the bowls. Then they all sat down and began eating quickly.

"This is much better than what I am usually served here." Peregrine commented.

"I used a recipe Groman taught me and that our mother taught him. It is all in the spices." Annie said with a smile.

"Speaking of that, how come you put a different spice in the farmer's bowl?" Dani asked.

Annie smiled wryly. "I do not know what you referring to." She giggled.

"You had better be careful doing that sort of thing in the future." A voice said behind her. Annie spun around, nearly spilling her stew in the process, to see the farmer's wife standing behind her with a pile of bread in her arms. "I know you added some polyhorit to Atrian's stew. That is why I am out here instead of in there. I do not want to be there when he tries..."

She was cut off by a loud shout followed by retching from inside the house. Saralia looked at Annie and laughed.

"Polyhorit? That is some strong stuff. Good for making someone like Trakken, stop from stealing food."

"Or a little revenge." Annie said with a wink towards Dani who looked surprised but managed a weak smile.

"I am sorry for the way my husband treated you. He can get very angry when his food is not ready when it wants it. I have found it is best to stay out of his way when he is in one of his moods. He has been angry ever since he broke his favorite pitchfork on those gritters earlier."

Dani didn't say anything but quietly finished her meal and then climbed up a wooden ladder to the hay loft.

Just then Tiny and the other unkarian walked in the barn.

"Where have you two been?" Stephen asked.

Tiny didn't say anything but walked over to the hay and sat down. The other unkarian walked over to the cauldron and quickly drained it like a bowl of soup before sitting down by the doorway.

"You did not answer the question Kearon. What were you up to?" The farmer's wife said firmly.

"We had a casual discussion in the field. That is all." Kearon said before looking outside the barn.

Stephen looked over at Tiny and noticed a small scar that was in the process of healing itself near Tiny's eye. Saralia seemed to notice it too and she walked over to Kearon.

"You did not have a discussion; you had a fight!" She said angrily. Kearon stood up and looked down at her.

"What if we did? It is not my fault that he is a nitwit and cannot walk right." Kearon coldly retorted. Annie gasped and looked over at Tiny who was looking down at the floor. Saralia looked up at the unkarian who was now looming over her.

"If you ask me. Tiny is the smartest one here because he is resisting the urge to throw you out of the barn right now. And if I were you, I would watch what I say. Some of us do not have the same restraint." Saralia growled before turning around and started to walk away.

Kearon laughed and walked up behind Saralia and purposely stepped on her long tail getting her to stop. "What are you going to do about it four legs?"

Saralia didn't say anything but kicked out with her hind legs, connecting with the unkarian's gut and sending him falling back against the frame of the barndoor.

"I did warn you." Saralia said with a flick of her tail as she walked back towards the others. Stephen and Jack started laughing at Kearon who was now stumbling out of the barn in embarrassment.

"We have been needing a better way to keep him in line. I may have to hire you too!" The farmer's wife chuckled as she started rolling the empty cauldron back to the house.

After she had left Jack climbed up the ladder into the hayloft where he found Dani sitting by an open window drawing in her sketchbook and staring out at the triple moons that lighted the night sky.

"It's just more proof." Dani said quietly.

"Of what?" Jack asked.

"That we really are somewhere different."

"I'd say so."

"If only the people were different too."

Dani closed her sketchbook and looked at Jack. She had tears running down her face and onto her dress. Jack walked over and sat down in the hay next to her.

"When he started yelling at me, I didn't even see him anymore. I just saw my dad in one of his drunken rages. Only this time I was armed. I was reaching for my dagger without even realizing what I was doing! It's like this time instead of just standing there and taking it, I was ready to fight back." Dani said quietly.

"But you didn't."

"No. I remembered something you said back when we dealt with those bullies in our woods. There is a time and place to fight, and sometimes we do need to stand up for ourselves and fight back, but not all of the time. We need to keep to the high road and follow what God says."

Jack put his arm around Dani and held her close to him. "I'm sorry Dani. I should have been there. I'll try to keep an eye out for you from now on."

"You couldn't have known. Besides, you can't be at my side every hour of every day. There are times where we both have to go it alone."

Jack sighed and nodded. He looked up at the three moons again and then towards the mountain range that lay in their way. He then reached into his pocket and pulled out his inhaler, looking it over in the moonlight.

"Have you told them yet?" Dani asked.

"No."

"When are you going to?"

"Only if I have to."

"Jack, you could get yourself hurt if you don't. Besides, you're only delaying the inevitable. They're sure to find out eventually."

"Only if I let them see it. This world is my chance to finally prove myself! I can actually do some good here!"

"Or die a fool for trying too hard. Please be careful."

Dani got up from the window, walked to the edge of the loft and then disappeared down the ladder. Jack looked back out the window once more and sighed.

"This is my chance to prove myself. Someway, somehow, I'll make you proud Dad."

Chapter 5. The Ascent.

Stephen and Saralia chatted while Annie unfolded her sleeping mat on the bed of hay. Victoria walked over to Tiny who was still sitting away from the group facing the wall. She quietly put her hand on his massive shoulder.

"Are you alright Tiny?" She asked softly.

"Tiny... Is fine." Tiny quietly replied.

"Do you want to tell me what happened?"

"Tiny trip over rock. Kearon call Tiny stupid. Tiny ignore Kearon and Kearon call Tiny coward and attack Tiny."

"I'm sorry Tiny, I should have been there."

"No Tiny alright. Tiny used to it."

"You shouldn't have to be."

"Make no difference. Tiny called stupid and dumb all Tiny's life. Like stream under bridge now."

Victoria awkwardly hugged Tiny's massive body and looked up at his face which was now starting to show a smile.

"If you say so. If you ever need to talk, I'm here."

"Thank you, Tori."

Victoria smiled and walked back to Stephen, who was now sitting on top of an old barrel, and Saralia who had just taken off her saddlebags and was attempting to get the last of the mud off her horse flanks.

"Did you hear that? He called me Tori!" Victoria said happily.

"He only says your name when he really wants to." Annie said as she walked over to the group. "He prefers to give everybody his own names."

"Like little soldier." Stephen said.

"Strong girl." Saralia said proudly.

"Pretty girl." Annie added with a giggle.

"So who does he call sword man?" Jack added as he climbed down from the hayloft. "I've heard him say it once or twice."

Annie frowned slightly. "He calls my brother Groman that because of his big sword."

"Oh, that makes sense." Jack responded as he walked over to the pile of bedrolls and picked one out for himself.

"Are you alright Annie?" Stephen asked sitting up on his mat. "I'm surprised you aren't more worried about Groman."

"I am well." Annie replied. "I am worried, but I know Groman can take care of himself and that The One Above is watching over both of us. I just miss him more than anything right now." Victoria gave Annie a hug and looked her in the eyes.

"We'll find him, don't worry."

Just then Dani and Peregrine walked into the barn. Dani's blond hair was messed up and she was grinning from ear to ear.

"Where did you go?" Jack asked.

"Peregrine took me for a ride in the moonlight. It was spectacular!"

"I was going to scout for any more gritters, and she wanted to go along." Peregrine said.

"You should really try it, Tori! It was amazing!" Dani said excitedly.

"I have, once. Falamore gave me a ride on my first visit." Victoria said quietly. "It was just a few days before he was killed in battle."

Peregrine gave Victoria a knowing look and walked back outside. Dani stayed quiet and walked over to Victoria.

"Sorry, I didn't mean anything." Dani said quietly.

"It's alright. You couldn't have known anyway." Victoria said. After a few minutes of uncomfortable silence Saralia stomped a front hoof on the ground and spoke up.

"We should try to get some sleep. We have a long climb ahead of us tomorrow." Saralia said as she knocked the last of the dried mud off her flanks.

"I agree, Jack and I will take the loft, everyone else can stay down here." Stephen said as he grabbed his mat and started climbing the ladder. Jack quickly followed and the two men bedded down for the night.

As they lay on their mats under some warm blankets, Stephen heard Jack tossing and turning in his bedroll.

"Not what you expected is it?" Stephen asked quietly.

Jack sighed before replying "Somewhat. I did expect what you had told me about, but I also expected a lot more adventuring and swordplay. It's been just walking and work so far."

"Swordplay? This coming from the guy who chose a crossbow as their main weapon?"

"I wanted a ranged weapon; your great aunt's sword was very nice but kinda heavy for me. I figured a crossbow, and a one-handed sword would be a bit more manageable."

"If you say so. Have you ever fired one of those things before?"

"Once at a relative's lodge. They're fairly simple to use, almost like a gun."

Stephen sighed and rolled away from Jack.

"Stephen, what do you think lies ahead of us?"

"Probably a day or two of climbing, another day of walking through the mountains, and then..." Stephen paused deep in thought.

"What?"

"I should ask Peri if she has any idea. Blackmians like her have incredible eyesight. Maybe she's been over them before?"

"I can tell you right now I have not." Peregrine's voice came from the window startling the two men.

"Peregrine? What are you doing?" Jack asked in surprise.

"I was just returning from another scouting flight when I heard my name, so I flew in closer to find out what was being said. And in case you are wondering the gritters have retreated for now."

"So do you have any idea about what is within or past the northern range?" Stephen asked.

Peregrine stepped in through the window and looked down at the two men.

"Not much, only what I have heard from other mercenaries. Some say that there are monsters beyond our imagination that live up there. Others say that there are entire civilizations tucked within the mountain tops. Still others say it is a desolate wasteland. I for one have not flown too close to those mountains due to the storms that tend to catch even the most seasoned climbers off guard. In any case I suggest you use caution."

Peregrine walked over to the ladder and started to climb down before Stephen stopped her.

"Will you come with us? We could use someone with your skills."

Peregrine looked at him with a look of mild sadness.

"I have debts that need to be paid soon, if I do not, things will be much worse for me than when we were in the ruined city. Unless you can promise that by helping to save your friend's brother, I will gain extraordinary wealth, I cannot help you. However, I do hope you find him. Although with his weapon and skills, I would not be surprised if he found you first."

Peregrine quickly slid down the ladder and disappeared from sight. Stephen laid back on his mat and wondered what was waiting for them tomorrow until the blessed arms of sleep finally took hold.

The next morning Stephen was awakened to the sound of a hammer hitting something metal. He looked over to see that Jack was already gone and the sunlight was just starting to come through the loft's window. Stephen quickly got up, rolled up his mat, and slid down the ladder into the ground floor of the barn. He found the farmer's wife was busy handing out fresh bread for their breakfast, Victoria was talking with Saralia, and Dani was helping Annie with her set of wooden legs.

"Good morning, Stephen!" Annie called out before she resumed hitting her wooden legs with a hammer.

"What are you doing? Don't you need those to walk?" Stephen asked in surprise as he hurried over.

"I am just putting some nails through the foot to help with the climb ahead." Annie responded cheerfully. "I could not do it with my metal ones and besides, those would get colder faster than my wooden ones."

Dani tossed the right leg to Stephen, and he caught it before quickly turning it over and seeing that Annie had pounded seven nails through the foot to act as climbing spikes, with four in the front and three in the back.

"I'd say it's a good idea." Stephen said handing Annie back the leg as she finished with the other.

Victoria was busy helping Saralia clip on her spiked horseshoes that snapped into place over her normal ones.

"I normally use these for ice fishing on Frost Lake, but these should work well on the mountain trails." Saralia said to Victoria as she snapped the last one into place.

"I've seen animals in our world wear something similar." Victoria commented. Just then Jack and Peregrine walked into the barn.

"Any gritters coming our way?" The farmer's wife asked as she handed them a still-steaming loaf.

"Not that I could see." Jack said.

"I do not think we will see any today. After the beating we gave them yesterday they should be staying well away for a while." Peregrine said before sinking her teeth into the bread. "Oh Stephen, while I was up there, I did take a look at the mountains, it looks like there is a small trail leading up the mountains just north of here." She said in between mouthfuls.

"So the stories are true." The farmer's wife mused.

"Stories?" Annie asked.

"When I was a little girl, I heard tales of strange folk that lived on the top of the northern range who would venture down a steep trail on rare occasion to trade. But after a while they stopped coming and nobody has heard from them since. A few have tried to climb the trail themselves, but those mountains are prone to sudden storms and only a handful have returned unscathed." The farmer's wife responded.

"Well I guess we will have to be the first to climb it then." Victoria said as she stood up from helping Saralia with her shoes.

"Indeed." Jack said quietly.

"Are you sure you want to go over those mountains?" Peregrine asked.

"Positive." Stephen answered firmly.

"We can make it." Dani said.

"I have no doubt that you will find Groman, or that maybe he will find you first."

"Thank you, Peregrine." Annie said.

Soon the travelers were ready to move on from the farm. Dani noticed that the farmer still hadn't shown himself as they made ready to leave. When she asked the farmer's wife she simply said. "He is not feeling well today" and no more. Before they left the farm Saralia handed out the cloaks that she had carried for everyone, and Tiny borrowed a large and rough blanket from the farm to keep his huge body warm as they pushed north. Then they departed from the farm and began to walk towards the mountains that now loomed overhead.

As they journeyed Stephen heard Peregrine's screech overhead and he turned around and saw her winged figure soaring through the sky.

He waved and he almost thought he saw her wave back as she wheeled about and turned back towards the farm.

After nearly an hour of walking they came to the entrance of the trail. It was a steep and narrow path that led up into the mountains ahead.

"Single file everyone." Jack said as he quickly took the lead and began climbing.

They all fell into line with Saralia, Victoria, Dani, Annie, Stephen, and Tiny bringing up the rear.

The trail was steep and rough but there were occasional spots where it leveled off and doubled back on itself in a switchback fashion. The group took time to rest when they needed to, Jack was finding it harder to breathe but he refrained from touching his inhaler, only using it when he was certain nobody would notice. After nearly four hours of climbing the group stopped at another spot where the trail leveled off to share some of the food that they had packed. As they ate, Victoria looked up and saw that there were some grey clouds moving in towards them from the north.

"We may need to find shelter soon, looks like there's a storm coming." She said.

"There's nothing around here, we need to keep moving forwards." Jack said as he quickly jumped up.

Soon they rounded a bend in the trail and Annie let out a squeal of delight and pushed past everybody.

"Snow!" She said as she rushed forwards and leapt into a small pile of snow that lay by the trail.

"I take it you haven't seen much of it before?" Dani said as she also hurried forward and grabbed a handful of the white powder.

"We do not get much of it in the woods. Only a few inches a year." Annie replied as she playfully threw a snowball at Dani who ducked, and the snowball hit Saralia's front. Saralia chuckled for a moment but then her face went firm.

"As much fun as a snow fight would be, we need to keep moving. If we are out in the open when a storm hits, we will need someone to save us instead." She said.

Annie's smile dropped and she nodded, dropping the freshly formed snowball she had just made. They returned to the trail which began to steepen as they pushed ever higher into the mountains. Soon they came to a large outcropping of stone to the side of the trail. There the group rested for a few minutes as the air began to thin and everybody, especially the humans and Annie, were beginning to feel its effects.

"How much farther?" Annie asked.

"I do not know." Saralia said as she unrolled a large horse blanket and put it on.

"Let's just rest here for a few minutes." Victoria said.

"I'm going to scout ahead." Jack said. "Maybe I'll find something useful."

"Alright but be careful." Stephen said.

Jack quickly left the rocky shelter and disappeared.

"Tiny not like heights." Tiny said quietly.

"Just don't look back." Dani said comfortingly.

Just then Jack returned with a worried look on his face.

"So, we may have a bit of a problem." He said.

"What do you mean?" Saralia asked.

"Come with me and you'll see." Jack replied.

The group left their shelter and moved up the trail to see what Jack was talking about. They soon saw the cause of his worry. It was very steep and narrow flight of stairs that was cut into a sheer rock ledge nearly fifteen feet tall.

"Tiny see no problem here." Tiny said as he backed up, got a running start, and jumped, just barely catching the top of the ledge before pulling himself up onto the top.

"Easy for you to say." Jack said.

"We can climb the stairs Jack; I don't see what the problem is." Dani said as she started to go up the narrow stairs. Jack, Victoria, Annie, and Stephen followed behind while Saralia watched nervously. The four of them had to turn slightly sideways in order to fit but they all were on the top of the cliff in short order.

"Can you make it up Saralia?" Victoria said turning around to look at their four-hoofed friend.

"Umm... Sure I can." Saralia said with a quiver in her voice. She went to put her front hooves on the first steps only to stop a second later.

"Well this is awkward." Stephen whispered before doubling over in pain as Victoria quickly elbowed him in the gut. Annie let out a giggle and Saralia turned a bright red as everybody saw that Saralia's lower half was slightly too wide to fit into the narrow stone steps.

"Now what do we do?" Dani asked.

"Even if she took off her weapons and saddlebags she wouldn't fit." Victoria added.

"You know I can hear you!" Saralia shouted turning an even brighter shade of red as she backed away from the steps.

"Tiny could carry you..." Stephen suggested before being cut off by Saralia who shouted.

"Absolutely not!"

"Strong girl too heavy for Tiny to jump onto cliff with." Tiny said.

"What did you just call me?" Saralia shouted again.

"You could try to toss her up here." Dani suggested.

"Cliff too high and strong girl might be hurt when landing." Tiny replied.

"I don't suppose you could jump up here?" Stephen asked.

"No." Saralia replied with an exasperated sigh.

"I knew this would happen." Jack said as he started pacing around the top of the ledge.

"There has to be a way. The farmer's wife mentioned that traders used to come through here. There's no way they would try to squeeze down those steps carrying things to trade with." Annie said.

Stephen looked around at their surroundings. The space above and below the ledge were fairly flat except for the ledge itself. But the area around them were sheer rock walls and cliffs much too steep for Saralia or anyone else to climb without proper equipment.

"What about that?"

Dani's voice broke Stephen's train of thought and he looked up to see what she was pointing at above them. Above them was a large rock outcropping that jutted out over the cliff.

"That may be sturdy enough to hold her." Stephen said to himself. "Does anyone have rope? The more the better!" He asked the rest of the group.

"I have quite a bit in my saddlebags, but you had better not be thinking what I think you are thinking!" Saralia shouted below them.

"It's either that or turn around!" Jack shouted as he and Dani started climbing down the stairs again.

Soon the two of them had made a makeshift harness around Saralia's horse half and tossed the rope over the rock outcropping. Tiny caught it and he, Jack, and Stephen started to slowly pull Saralia up the cliff.

"The One Above, this is so humiliating." Saralia grumbled as her four legs left the ground and she was hoisted into the air. Soon her head and shoulders cleared the top of the ledge and Victoria and Dani were there to gently pull the rest of her over the top. Suddenly Jack noticed the outcropping was beginning to crack under Saralia's weight.

"Hurry! That outcropping isn't going to last long!" he shouted.

Annie raced over and grabbed the rope around Saralia's back and dug her spiked feet in and pulled with all her strength. In a few seconds the outcropping gave way just as everyone pulled with one accord and Saralia toppled to the ground landing on her right side. The rest of the party fell on their backsides and Annie's legs were pinned under Saralia's horse half. Saralia let out a shout of pain and quickly scrambled to get back on all four hooves again. Victoria looked over and saw several small, bleeding gashes in the horse blanket where the spikes on Annie's prosthetic legs had accidentally cut their friend.

"I am so sorry Saralia!" Annie said as she struggled to her feet.

"I will be fine." Saralia said as she dusted herself off. "I brought healing herbs for a reason."

"No need herbs, Tiny here." Tiny said as he walked over to Saralia and held out his hands.

"Watch this." Stephen whispered to Jack and Dani.

The rest of the group watched as Tiny closed his eyes and whispered a prayer before laying his hands on Saralia's wounds. After a few seconds Tiny stepped back with a sigh and sat down looking very tired. Dani couldn't believe her eyes when she saw that the wounds were completely gone, the only evidence of them even having been there in the first place were a few spots of drying blood and the cuts in Saralia's horse blanket.

"So that's how he did it." Victoria murmured.

Saralia shook out her tail and looked the rest of the group.

"We will not speak of this ever again. Or By The One Above I will personally throw any or all of you into the Ice River!" She said coldly before moving up the trail once more. The group quickly followed her and continued to climb ever higher into the mountains. Soon they noticed the dark cloud seemed only a few feet above them and the temperature was dropping quickly.

"Is it just me, or is it starting to snow?" Dani called out from the back of the group.

"It's snowing alright. We need to keep going." Victoria replied.

Soon the snow began to fall in larger amounts and the wind started to pick up speed. The group pushed on until they were inside the storm clouds. They could barely see anything around them due to thick fog and the snow.

"Hold up!" Jack shouted as the group came to a stop. "We should tie ourselves together with rope, so nobody gets lost in this storm!"

Victoria quickly ran up to Saralia and pulled out the rope and made a loop around her waist and then handed the rest to Saralia who tied it to her sword belt and handed it to Annie who was next in line. Soon they were all tied together with Victoria in the lead. The higher they went the more snow they encountered as even more continued to fall.

Victoria held her hands in front of her face, trying to shield her eyes from the now blinding snowstorm when she felt a sharp tug around her waist.

"What's going on back there?" She tried to shout but the noise of the storm drowned out her voice. Feeling the rope loosen she started walking up the trail again when suddenly a deafening roar echoed around her.

"Hurry!" a voice screamed behind her as she could feel the slack in the rope as Saralia started to run, dragging Annie behind her. Victoria did her best to sprint but kept slipping on the heavy snow. Suddenly she was met with a blinding light, and she stopped for a few seconds and let her eyes adjust. She saw that she had literally walked out of the storm, and she could see the clouds only a few feet below her. Ahead of her the path leveled out and she saw what looked like a large village in the distance.

"Pull!" Saralia's voice boomed behind her.

Victoria turned around and saw Saralia and Annie were tugging on the rope with every ounce of strength they had left.

"What happened?" Victoria asked as she joined the others in pulling the rope.

"Avalanche! It buried everyone else behind me!" Annie shouted.

"We have to pull them out quickly!" Saralia said.

The girls kept pulling and soon Jack emerged from the snowbank covered in the white powder.

"Who was after you?" Saralia asked gasping for breath in the now thin air.

"Tiny." Jack managed to wheeze before collapsing on the ground.

The girls grabbed the rope behind Jack and kept tugging.

"He's too heavy we need more help!" Victoria gasped. She could feel herself running out of air quickly. Then she heard a bell start to ring behind her, she glanced over her shoulder as dozens of tall, white figures emerged from seemingly everywhere and started to rush towards them. She let go of the rope and reached for her weapons but felt herself lose consciousness as the tall figures covered in white fur stepped over her and peered down at her. The last thing she saw was Annie's face looking down at her frantically trying to wake her up before everything went black.

Chapter 6. Testing.

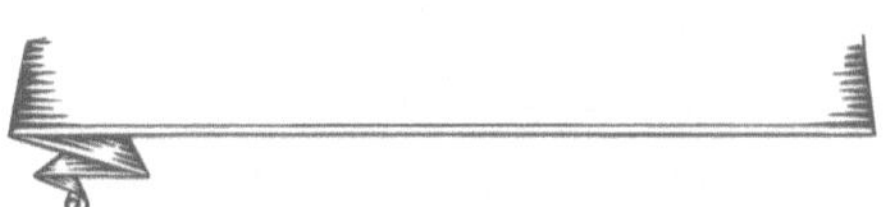

Stephen felt his senses return with a jolt. The last thing he remembered was trying to run from a wall of white when his legs gave out and he fell only to have Tiny try to shield him and get knocked away by the snow and ice. Stephen kept his eyes closed and tried to feel his surroundings. He was under something soft and warm, but he knew that feeling warm could mean he was in the opening stages of hypothermia and was now freezing to death. He could feel his arms and legs and he even wiggled his fingers and toes to make sure nothing was broken. Then he felt what was on his face being removed and then something or someone was breathing on him. Thinking he had been dug out of the snowbank he opened his eyes and let out a scream. There was indeed someone looking at him, but it was unlike anything he had ever seen before.

The creature's face was covered in white fur, it had small black eyes, a tiny nose, a narrow mouth, and black goat-like horns jutting out from its head. The creature let out a surprised shout of its own and then tried to hold Stephen down. Stephen summoned what little strength he had and grabbed at his attacker only to feel another creature pin his arms to what he now knew was a bed. Stephen kept shouting to for them to let him go but their arms were like iron now and he was nearly out of breath in the thin mountain air.

He heard Dani shout from across the room.

"Stephen stop! They're friends!"

"Calm down boy! You are safe here!" Another voice shouted.

Stephen let himself rest again and the two creatures released him and stepped back from his bed. Stephen slowly sat up and quickly felt his head begin throbbing with an unmatched intensity. He lay back down and closed his eyes, and he felt the pain lessen a little bit. He felt a human hand on his arm, and he opened his eyes to see Dani's face looking at him with a concerned expression.

"You got hit in the head with some chunks of ice. You need to relax now." Dani said quietly.

"Where's my sister and Tiny?" Stephen managed to whisper.

"Tori is recovering in another room and Tiny is in a barn nearby, unconscious but healing."

"Where are we?"

"I don't really know; I came to myself a less than an hour ago. I heard you shouting, and I hurried over to make sure you were alright. I was buried in the snow like almost everyone else."

"You are in the village known as Iceborne, home of the Ibexian tribe." A voice spoke up.

Stephen slowly sat up again, ignoring the searing pain in his head and looked to see who had spoken. He saw a tall figure covered in white fur walking towards him with the aid of a wooden staff. Other than a leather strap over its shoulder it was only covered in its long white fur. It reminded Stephen of that brown-furred creature in a science fiction movie he had seen except for the black goat-like horns, small black eyes, and a mouth that stuck out slightly like a muzzle of a goat.

"Who are you?" Stephen gasped as he laid back down on his bed.

"I am chief Glarion. Leader of this village." The old Ibexian said calmly. "We heard your friend's call for help after the storm passed and my people have dug you all out and given you medicine for your injuries."

"Thank you, sir." Dani replied. "We couldn't have gotten out of that snowbank without your help. If there is any way for us to repay your kindness, please just say the word."

"I would ask what brings a group of lowlanders into our mountain city?" Glarion asked as he sat down on a stone chair.

"We are trying to cross the northern range to find a missing friend who was carried off by some raiders." Stephen answered.

"And you think they went north?"

"All we know is that they were last spotted flying north towards this mountain range." Dani replied.

"Well, a few of my people reported hearing someone calling for help during the night a few days ago."

"What?" Stephen said quickly sitting up only to moan in pain and fall back against the pillows. Dani pulled a warm cloth out of a bucket of water and laid it on Stephen's head. The chief stood up slowly and walked over towards the door before looking back at Stephen and Dani.

"We would have tried to help but we do not leave our houses after dark or during storms." The chief replied. "I will send my healers to check on you in an hour or so. When you are feeling better you are welcome to stay in the village, I only ask that you stay inside after sundown and during the storms. As you will be staying here for a while, I will see about clearing a house for you and your friends."

"We won't stay that long. We only need to recover, and we will be on our way again." Dani said quietly.

"I am afraid once you arrive in our village you cannot leave. Not until it is killed." Glarion said as he left the room.

"Now what have we gotten ourselves into?" Stephen sighed.

"I don't know. Hopefully it's nothing we can't handle." Dani replied. "You should get some rest now. Someone will come back to check on you later."

Stephen slowly nodded and he closed his eyes and tried to rest. Dani quietly tiptoed out of the room and into the stone hallway. She walked over to the next room and knocked on the door.

"Come in."

Hearing Annie's reply from inside Dani quietly opened the door and slipped into the room. It was very much like Stephen's room with stone walls and a high ceiling. A fireplace stood at the back of the room and Dani saw two figures huddled in front of it, one of whom was wrapped in a large blanket.

"How are you doing Tori?" Dani asked as she sat down beside her friend.

"Still trying to warm up." Victoria replied with a quiver in her voice. "But I'm alright."

"I think my ankle may be broken." Annie said reaching under her dress and pulling off her right prosthetic leg.

"Looks fine to me." Dani remarked.

"I think the joint is slightly bent." Annie remarked as she moved the wooden foot back and forth. The three girls sat in silence for a few minutes before Annie spoke up.

"Did the chief talk to you too?" she asked.

"Yes. He told us that we will not leave until 'it' is killed." Dani replied.

"What do you think 'it' is?" Victoria asked.

"I honestly have no clue. The farmer's wife mentioned something about monsters living up in these mountains, but those Ibexians seem to be very strong, surely they can kill a monster or two." Annie replied.

"I agree but that only means that if there is something that they can't handle it must be a creature unlike anything we have fought before." Victoria said.

"We can do it. There are seven of us not to mention Tiny's raw strength and Saralia being expert huntress. We should be fine." Dani remarked before sliding closer to her two friends in front of the fire.

Jack slowly got up from his bed and looked around at the room he was in. His goat-like doctor had left him alone nearly fifteen minutes ago and he was anxious to get out of there. He looked around for his weapons and soon spotted his sword lying beside the doorframe. After strapping it on he glanced around for his crossbow and saw it and its quiver hanging by a roaring fireplace. He armed himself and quietly crept towards the door. He peeked out into the dimly lit, stone hallway and made sure the coast was clear before making his way down the passageway towards what he hoped would be the way out. As he silently walked, he heard someone shout and the sound of metal hitting stone coming from a door to his right. He notched an arrow on the string of his crossbow and gingerly opened the door to peer inside. Inside he saw Saralia pacing around a very large room, it was her metal horseshoes making the clatter he had heard from outside. Jack pulled the arrow out of the crossbow and released the string which snapped forwards with a twang. Saralia quickly looked over at Jack and trotted over to him with a look of relief on her face.

"Jack! Thank The One Above! I am glad to see you are well! I was beginning to worry! Have you seen the others?" Saralia asked.

"No, you're the first familiar face I've seen since I passed out." Jack replied. He heard a loud snore coming from the corner of the room. He looked over and saw Tiny slumped in the corner of the room sleeping peacefully. "Is Tiny alright?" he asked.

"He will be fine. His wounds have healed but he is exhausted as a result, so he will be sleeping for a while yet." Saralia replied. "Unkarians can heal quickly, however it puts a lot of strain on their bodies."

"Makes sense. So, what do we do now?"

"I do not know. Those creatures, I think they are called Ibexians, told me to wait here until they return." Saralia replied.

"Are they friendly?"

"It would appear so, but I would not trust them as far as I could throw them."

"You think they have something sinister in mind for us?"

"That could be, it could be similar to the bedtime stories I have heard from my mother and Trakken."

"Well we'd better play it safe, if we do anything drastic, we'd be heavily outnumbered in seconds."

"I agree."

Just then a knock was heard at the door and one of the Ibexians peered inside.

"Aha! I found the low lander! He is in here!" the creature shouted back into the hallway.

Soon the Ibexian entered the room followed by the rest of Jack's friends and an older Ibexian walking with a long staff. Once they were all inside the Ibexian with a staff gestured for the other Ibexian to leave which it promptly did.

"I am chief Glarion, you are most welcome to my village, your friends have told me about your quest to find a missing friend. However, I have to inform you that your quest is at an end. You can go no further than this humble city known as Iceborne." The old creature said quietly.

"Why not?" Jack asked in surprise.

"Are you keeping us as prisoners?" Saralia nearly shouted.

"Our village was once alive with trades and commerce from the lowlands around us but now a terrifying beast has kept us trapped for a very long time. It is known as the Cliff Crawler Queen. It likes to attack the outskirts of the village after nightfall or during snowstorms with its young. While its young are formidable and can be killed by a skilled hunter, the queen is another monster entirely. Our ancestors killed the first one in an epic hunt that went on for weeks. Many of the finest warriors were killed by it before it was finally brought down. However, our ancestors knew that one day another would return and have declared that only the strongest, fastest, and smartest warriors could be allowed to fight it to keep more lessor hunters from wasting their lives. They devised a test for each criterion and yet and none of our warriors have passed. So, we have decided to wait for the Cliff Crawler Queen to live out its life without our attempting to kill it in order for our people to not give their lives in vain. Until the tests are completed, we cannot allow anyone to hunt the queen."

"We can do it!" Victoria said quickly. "We've taken on bigger things than this monster before!"

"We have the skills and the knowhow!" Stephen said. "Just tell us where to go and we'll rid your city of this threat!"

"Only if you or your friends can pass any of the three tests will we allow you to attempt such a dangerous task." Glarion said.

"I am the fastest and strongest one here! I am certain I can beat whatever tests you have for me!" Saralia said rearing up on her hind legs and landing with a loud thud.

Tiny stirred and lifted his head. "No, Tiny stronger, Tiny take test for strong girl." He said before letting his head fall back on his chest and resuming his snoring.

"He is not wrong Saralia." Annie said with a giggle.

"The One Above... Very well." Saralia sighed. She stomped a front hoof and crossed her arms. "I am still faster though." She said with a huff.

"I guess that leaves the test for the smartest." Jack said.

"That would be me." Stephen said stepping forward.

"Are you sure?" Victoria asked.

"I bet Jack could do it." Dani replied.

"I'm pretty sure I outclass him in that regard." Stephen said with a smirk.

"Steve, you didn't need to say it like that." Victoria said elbowing her twin brother.

"Yeah, I bet he's got more battle strategy's, tactics, and history memorized than anyone else I know." Dani said as she put her hands on her hips and scowled.

"I know an easy way of settling this." Jack said stepping forwards.

"Oh? What's that?" Victoria asked.

"A challenge to single combat?" Saralia suggested.

"Not quite." Jack said as he stepped towards Stephen who slowly reached for his sword. Jack stopped in front of Stephen and held out a clenched fist. "Rock, paper, scissors." He said with a smile.

Stephen smiled and held out his own fist. "I accept your challenge."

The two men shook their fists and shouted, "Rock, Paper, Scissors!" When the shouting stopped Stephen held two fingers like a pair of scissors while Jack's was still a tightly clenched fist. Stephen looked on in shock before looking to Victoria for support. She simply giggled at her brother's defeat and winked at Jack.

"Best out of three?" Stephen whimpered.

"Nope." Jack chuckled. "Looks like I have a test to get ready for."

Stephen sighed rather loudly and turned away sulking. Just then elder Glarion came back inside the room and looked over the group with a smile.

"You have decided to undertake the tests, yes?" Glarion asked.

"We want to help and if this is the only way for us to cross the mountains, we're in." Victoria said.

"Very well. The tests will begin when you are accustomed to the thinner air. When you are ready, the test of speed will take place first. Until then you are welcome guests in our humble village. You will have rooms and everything you need provided. For now, feel free to get some more rest. You will need to save your strength for the trials ahead."

Chapter 7. Speed, Strength, and Intelligence.

In the following week the seven adventurers spent their time getting acclimated to the thin air on the top of the mountains and making plans on what they were to do once they passed the tests and could continue on. Saralia, Tiny, and Jack spent time training as well as they could to be ready for the trials ahead. On the day of the first test the group met together in the large room where Saralia was staying. Saralia was trotting around the room warming up for her challenge while the others stood in the middle out of her way.

"Are you ready Sara?" Victoria asked.

"I am more than ready now." Saralia huffed as she came to a stop by her friends. "I am warmed up and I have the sweat to prove it. Not that I have a major challenge in front of me. I can easily outrun everyone here and those Ibexians are no different."

"I don't know Saralia, If it's a race then why did they give you wooden swords?" Jack asked, pointing to the two wooden weapons that hung at her sides.

"He's right." Dani added. "Something doesn't seem right."

"If there is fighting involved it makes no difference whether I am fighting at full gallop or standing still." Saralia said crossing her arms.

Stephen opened his mouth to say something but was cut off by a loud voice coming from behind them.

"Challenger Saralia, are you ready for the test of speed?" Glarion's voice echoed in the stone chamber.

"By The One Above I know I am ready." Saralia said firmly.

"Then my warriors will take you to the arena." Glarion said as he motioned for two Ibexian warriors to step forward. Stephen noticed that they were both carrying wooden staffs instead of the normal spears and swords he saw the guards were normally armed with. Saralia quickly trotted over to the warriors who led her out of the room. Glarion then beckoned for the rest of the party to come to him.

"Come, we will see how you friend fares in the challenge ahead." He said before leading the group through the stone passageway and out into the bright sunlit town.

Dani looked around at the village covered in a fresh layer of fine snow. The house were large structures built up against the surrounding mountainsides with small windows and many chimneys from which trails of smoke wafted into the clear blue sky. The houses were connected by rough stone paths that wound around the rocky terrain. There were paths that led up to small terraces that held small gardens covered by slanted roofs. A little further down one path she saw what looked to be a small forest populated by small evergreen trees with a large lumber yard nearby. She could see hundreds of Ibexians leaving their houses and moving towards a large stone structure that reminded her of the colosseum. She could hear shouts and cheers coming from within and knew that the entire village was there to watch.

The Chief led the group towards the large arena and towards a flight of stairs where he halted.

"I am afraid your large friend will have to enter the main gate; he is too big for my personal box." The chief said with a chuckle.

Tiny's face fell but he nodded in understanding and followed the crowds inside the gate. The chief then led the group up a flight of stairs and into a large comfortable seating area set a few stories above the arena floor.

From his vantage point Stephen surveyed the arena floor and felt his heart sink. He saw not a racecourse, but a large area, about one hundred feet square, staked out in the middle of the dirt field.

"It's not a race." He said to himself.

"What do you mean?" Annie asked as she stood beside him.

Stephen was about to answer when the chief walked over to the edge of the box and raised his arms to silence the arena.

"People of Iceborne! The time has come for the test of speed! Bring out the challenger!" The chief's voice echoed in the stone arena.

Victoria watched as a gate opened and Saralia rocketed out at full gallop and skidded to a halt near the square. A look of confusion came over her face, but she regained her composure and quickly reared up on her hind legs and leapt into the square drawing her wooden weapons and waving them about. The crowds roared their approval of Saralia's show while her friends looked on with concern as six Ibexian warriors all wielding wooden staffs also entered the ring and surrounded Saralia who's face turned to one of slight worry as the warriors never let their gaze leave her.

"In order for the challenger to pass the test they must defeat six of our best warriors before the water flows out of the great stone basin!" The chief said while gesturing to an enormous stone funnel filled with water. At the bottom of the funnel was a single Ibexian holding a rope attached to a plug at the bottom. Just below that was a chute that would take the water outside of the arena.

"Is the challenger ready?" Glarion asked.

"I was born ready!" Saralia's voice boomed back.

"The let the challenge begin!"

With that the Ibexian pulled the plug and water began to rush out. In the same moment four of the warriors leapt towards Saralia, two in front of her and two behind her. Saralia quickly blocked the attacks to her front with her weapons and kicked out with her hind legs. One of the warriors managed to leap away the other wasn't as lucky as he was sent flying out of the ring.

"That's one down." Jack said.

The two warriors in front of Saralia kept their weapons locked with hers as another warrior approached her left side. He managed to land a single hit before Saralia swung her hindquarters around and knocked the warrior down but not out of the ring. The two warriors that were in front of her let out a goat-like shout and attacked again locking their weapons. Saralia snorted and a large cloud of mist came from her nostrils as she began to twist her weapons around to get a more favorable angle for disarming the two fighters. The audience roared their approval as Saralia disarmed the two attackers, grabbing one of them and hurling him out of the ring as well.

"Two down, four to go." Stephen said.

"How much time does she have left?" Annie said worriedly.

"I'd guess only a few minutes at the most." Jack replied.

"Come on guys! Stay positive!" Victoria shot back.

"You can do it Saralia!" Dani cheered.

The four remaining warriors spread out standing by each of Saralia's four legs and no matter how fast she turned they kept pace with her. In one moment, they dropped their weapons and lunged at her legs. Saralia swung low with her weapons, but the warriors ducked lower. Together the warriors grabbed her by the legs and lifted her into the air. Saralia thrashed about and hit the two holding her front legs with her weapons, but they held firm and tossed her out of the ring where she landed on her side in the dirt. The audience cheered and the four warriors solemnly stepped out of the ring. One of them walked over to Saralia and offered her his hand to help her up. She pushed it away and quickly stood up and limped out of the arena. The chief then stood up and raised his arms to silence the arena.

"The test of speed has been failed, but all hope is not lost! The test of strength begins tomorrow!"

"Now what do we do?" Dani asked quietly after the chief spoke.

"You can all return to your rooms and see to your friend. The next test begins tomorrow" The chief responded as he walked out of the room.

"We should probably hurry I saw Saralia was limping when she left." Annie said.

The group quietly left the arena, collected a very solemn Tiny, and together they walked back to where Saralia was staying. When they entered her room, they saw Saralia lying down in a corner and softly crying, her face in her hands.

"Alright men, this is ladies' work. Go to Tiny's room and wait for us there." Victoria said firmly as she pushed the men back out into the hall and shut the large double doors.

Stephen turned around and faced Jack and Tiny.

"We need to plan for your tests. What we've seen today is that they aren't going to be as straight-forward as we had hoped."

Jack and Tiny nodded and the three of them quietly walked down the hall towards Tiny's room.

Back inside Saralia's room the three girls approached Saralia who was still quietly crying in the corner.

"Annie check Saralia's saddlebags for the healing herbs while Dani and I see how bad her hind leg is." Victoria said quietly. Annie nodded and quickly hurried over to the saddlebags that had been left in a corner and started looking through them. Victoria and Dani walked over to Saralia and put their hands on her shoulders.

"You're going to have to stand up so we can take a look at your leg." Dani said softly.

Saralia slowly stood up and raised her right hind leg in the air. Victoria took her hoof in her hands and examined it.

"I don't see any injuries just a bit of swelling around the hock. You must have landed on something hard, but I'm pretty sure you'll live." She said with a chuckle.

"It still hurts all the same." Saralia grumbled.

"Annie if you would, get some ice from outside and wrap it in a cloth and we can see about getting the swelling down." Dani replied.

Annie nodded and hurried out of the doorway. Victoria let go of Saralia's hoof and watched her friend lay down once again. She and Dani walked around Saralia and sat down on either side of her. After a few minutes of silence Saralia spoke up.

"They cheated me. The One Above! They said it was a test of speed, not combat."

"It's ok Sara, if anything we should have known something was up and given you better warning." Victoria responded.

"Yeah, and as the chief said, all hope isn't lost yet. Tiny gets to take his test tomorrow and Jack after that. I'm sure one of them will pass and then we can take care of that monster and be on our way." Dani chimed in.

"But it was supposed to be my victory! I am the fastest on this mountain! There is not anyone here who would argue with that!" Saralia shouted as she stood up and started to stomp around the room.

"You're right, nobody would argue with that." Victoria started to say but Saralia cut her off.

"Then why did I fail?" she shouted back.

"Because the test was something you weren't ready for. And even though you gave it a valiant effort, you couldn't do it. I'm sure if we had known and could have prepared for it you would have had a good chance. But for now, what's done is done and there isn't anything we can do about it except hope that Tiny and Jack pass their tests." Dani replied.

Saralia stopped pacing and looked back at her friends and sighed. "You are right. I did all I could do. I just need some time to think."

"And time you shall have, after I put some ice on that bruise." Annie said as she entered the doorway, a chunk of ice in hand. Victoria and Dani quietly left the room while Annie set about treating Saralia's bruised leg. The two of them walked down the stone hallway and stopped in front of a large set of double doors. Dani knocked on the door and Jack quickly opened one of them for the girls who entered the large room. They saw Tiny sitting in a corner dozing off, with Stephen pacing around the room.

"Well have you figured out what Tiny's test will be tomorrow?" Victoria asked.

"Not quite. It's a test of strength but after today's showing it's easy to see that the tests won't be as clear cut as we hoped." Jack answered.

"I think I have it narrowed down to two options." Stephen replied as he stopped his pacing.

"Let's hear them." Dani said.

"The first is that it will be what it says. A test of raw physical strength." Stephen began.

"If that's the case Tiny would have no problem with it." Victoria said.

"The second is that the strength mentioned is strength other than physical, like mental strength." Stephen finished.

"I keep thinking it could be willpower." Jack added.

"Why willpower?" Dani asked.

"Well, these tests are for the fastest, strongest, and smartest warriors who will go out and hunt a dangerous monster. Right?" Jack asked. The rest of the group nodded, and Jack continued. "The speed test was not a race it was about defeating a larger number of opponents before they got you. Now what did they tell us about the cliff crawler queen?"

"That it would attack the village at night or during snowstorms." Stephen started.

"With its brood!" Dani finished.

"Right, so there could be a time where the hunter could be surrounded by the young cliff crawlers and have to finish them quickly either before they are overwhelmed, or the mother shows up." Jack added.

"That kinda makes sense. But what about the next tests? How would they factor in?" Victoria asked.

"I'm guessing the strength test will be a test of will power as sometimes you need to focus on the main target and ignore the smaller easier targets. But that's really all I can think of. As for the test of intelligence I'm still not certain of anything right now." Jack answered.

"Well we may as well be ready for it if that is what the test is going to be." Stephen said as he walked over to Tiny and patted his enormous arm. "Hey, Tiny, did you hear all that?"

Tiny stirred awake and looked down at Stephen and smiled. "Tiny hear, but Tiny not sure what friends say."

"Tiny when they come to take you for your test you must do exactly what they tell you no matter what happens." Jack explained. "If they tell you to hold a door closed, you hold that door closed. If they tell you to push a cart."

"Tiny push the cart. Tiny understand now." Tiny said finishing Jack's sentence with a big smile.

"I guess that settles it then. I'm going back to my room." Victoria said with a yawn. The rest of the group nodded their agreement and left. Tiny started to doze off again when a voice stirred him awake again.

"Tiny. Can I talk to you?" Dani asked quietly.

Tiny looked down at the little girl and with one motion scooped her into the palm of his big hand.

"Annie said I could talk to you if I needed someone to talk to." Dani said quietly.

"Tiny know. Pretty girl told Tiny that you had bad time at farm." Tiny replied in a soft voice.

"She did huh? Well did she say what happened?"

"You make mistake, farmer got mad, you got reminded of bad time."

"So she did tell you."

"Not all, a small bit, Tiny fill in rest. Tiny know how it feels."

"You do?"

"Tiny's father was not nice unkarian, only nice unkarian was Tiny's mother."

"You do know, don't you?"

Tiny let out a big sigh and closed his eyes.

"Tiny's father not like Tiny, thought Tiny was stupid and slow. He try to hurt Tiny but Tiny's mother protect Tiny. Then Tiny's mother died, and Tiny's father found special sword and became evil monster. Tiny try to hide from other unkarians but was found and made to fight. All the time Tiny was made fun of and beaten because Tiny was different. Then one day big battle, Tiny captured and spared by little girl, Tiny helped little girl when Tiny's father hurt her badly. Now Tiny friends with everyone, but Tiny's past still has scars. But Tiny not like to think about past, Tiny look at future and how Tiny can help as many people as Tiny can."

Dani paused for a few minutes after hearing Tiny's story. She considered the similarities to her own life. Her own mother's disappearance, her abusive alcoholic father, and the bullies who tended to make her their target. Her life was very rough until Jack and his family came along. When her father went too far and was arrested, they took her in and Jack helped her deal with her bullies. But while those old wounds had healed, their scars still remained.

"You're right Tiny. I can't keep focusing on my past. I need to look to the present and future. While there are days my scars hurt, I can count on God and my friends to carry me through." Dani said quietly.

Tiny smiled and set Dani back on the ground again.

"Tiny know The One Above can help friends through anything. Tiny and friends only have to ask Him."

Dani nodded in agreement and walked to the doorway. Tiny lay against the wall and settled in for another nap.

"Tiny?" Dani asked quietly.

Tiny's massive form moved as he looked up at Dani.

"Annie was right, you are wiser than you look." She said with a smile.

Tiny's smile widened as he lay down and soon began snoring. Dani walked quietly back to her room hoping that her new giant friend would pass his test tomorrow.

The next morning Stephen, Victoria, Jack, Dani, and Annie were awakened by Ibexian guards and escorted to a lavish breakfast affair in a large meeting hall. The five of them were seated together at their own table but Stephen couldn't shake the feeling something seemed off.

"Does anyone else feel uneasy or is it just me?" he asked between mouthfuls of what he hoped were sausages.

"What do you mean?" Dani asked.

"Well for one thing as anybody heard from the chief about when Tiny's test will start?" Stephen replied.

"Now that you mention it, I have not seen Tiny since last night. And he never misses breakfast. He eats enough for all of us combined." Annie replied.

"Also, there is a sixth-place set at this table but only five chairs." Stephen added.

"Steve have you ever seen a trodontian use a chair?" Victoria asked, obviously annoyed by her brother who turned a faint shade of red with the realization of his error.

"Besides the fact that Saralia, who has also not shown up yet, doesn't need a chair wouldn't they have a place set for Tiny as well?" Stephen asked.

"Maybe he is getting prepared for his test right now and will join us later. I can't say the same for Saralia though." Jack responded.

"Well Saralia said she wanted some time to herself for now when I checked on her this morning before coming here." Annie answered.

"Do you think we should ask the chief where Tiny is?" Dani asked looking over to where the chief sat with whom she guessed were his wife and family. She noticed that while everyone else was eating at the chief's table and a few others had not even been served yet. Before she could think about it the large double doors at one end of the hall burst open and Tiny stumbled through. He was carrying a massive tray of food the size of an entire dinner table above his head and trying desperately to keep his balance as nearly a dozen Ibexian children were ramming their heads into his knees and ankles trying to upset his delicate load. Annie and Dani gasped while Stephen and Victoria nearly jumped up from their places, but Jack quickly spoke up.

"If this is the test we cannot interfere. We need to trust Tiny to pass without our help." Jack said quietly.

Stephen frowned but sat back down with Victoria following suit. Dani watched as Tiny carefully set the massive tray down on an empty table near where the chief and his family sat and began to serve them, all the while the Ibexian kids continued their head-butting assault. Tiny paid them no mind even when one or two of them managed to land a particularly hard hit with their goat-like horns. When Tiny finished serving the chief and his family, he collected the used bowls and plates on the tray and made his way back out of the hall once again. Throughout the rest of the meal the adventurers watched as Tiny served three other tables while under constant assault from the kids. When the meal was over the adventurers were escorted back to their rooms and shut in. Nearly six hours later they were joined by Saralia and brought back to the great hall once more for another feast and they saw that Tiny was still waiting tables with the kids never letting up their attacks. After serving two tables Tiny walked past the group and he managed a smile as he passed them. But that wasn't all that they noticed with Tiny.

"Did you hear that rumble? It sounded like an earthquake!" Dani asked.

"It sounded like Trakken's stomachs aching when he is really hungry." Saralia nonchalantly said while downing a bowl of stew.

"You don't think they are letting Tiny go hungry too, do you?" Victoria asked.

"I do not know but I do know a way to find out." Annie said as she got up from the table.

"Annie we can't interfere with the tests." Victoria responded.

"Do not worry they will not even know I was there." Annie said with a wink as she completely vanished into thin air. "Did you forget I can do this?" her disembodied voice said with a giggle. "I will be back soon."

"Jack, have you heard anything about when your test will be?" Stephen asked.

"No but one of the guards who escorted me hinted that it would be soon." Jack replied.

"Are you ready for it?" Dani asked.

"I'm ready for anything." Jack answered quickly.

The table of adventurers sat and ate quietly until a grinning Annie suddenly reappeared at her place again.

"Well, how is Tiny doing?" Victoria quickly asked.

"He is fine. I tried to offer him some food, but he told me it was part of his test to not eat so he refused. I know he is going to pass." Annie said with a big smile.

Saralia gave a slight look of disapproval but said nothing. Then they saw Tiny enter once again carrying another tray full of smoked meat. The adventurers could see he was sorely tempted by his load and the Ibexian kids were still at their game. Tiny came over to a table and set the tray down. Just as he did so the chief stood up and raised his hands to silence the room.

"Attention everyone! I hope you have enjoyed the test of strength feast today!" The chief shouted. Applause and cheers echoed around the room and the chief waited until it quieted down before he beckoned to Tiny who stepped towards him as the Ibexian kids scattered. "Tiny, mighty warrior of the lowlands. I must admit I had little doubt in your strength. Both physical and in will, and I am pleased to report you have passed the test of Strength!"

At this the whole hall erupted into applause and cheering as Tiny took a knee before the chief in respect. The adventurers stood from their table and joined in the cheering and applause. After a few minutes the chief raised his hands again to quiet the room.

"Tiny you may now join your companions at their table and eat your fill starting with the tray of meat you just now brought in." the chief said with a smile. Tiny grinned and picked up the tray and hurried over to his friends. After a happy lunch the group were allowed to roam the village once more and they enjoyed the fresh mountain air and a new layer of snow. Stephen attempted to start a snowball fight by lobbing one at Victoria. He missed and hit Annie in the back. She let out a shout of surprise and then pointed at Stephen who was quickly buried up to his neck in snow by Tiny. As he was digging Stephen out Jack saw an Ibexian guard walking over to the group.

"Challenger Jack, I am here to take you to your challenge this evening." The guard said firmly.

"Alright then. Let's go." Jack said confidently. He looked back at his friends who had just freed Stephen from his snow prison.

"Good luck Jack!" Dani called out.

"Let's make it two out of three!" Victoria shouted.

Jack smiled and then followed the guard back to the large arena where Saralia had taken her test the day before. He was led into a large armory where he saw his crossbow, sword, and dagger as well as a spear, club, and shield laying on a large worktable.

"I'm going to assume that this means my test will not be what I expected." Jack said looking over.

"That depends on what you expected." The guard replied coldly. "You are to choose one of these weapons to use in your test. You may also have your dagger as well."

Jack surveyed the table quietly and considered his options. He knew that since he didn't know what the test entailed, he had to figure out what he could make the most use of. The sword was a reliable weapon only he had no proper training, the club was useful only if he knew he was going to be able to get close to whatever he could be fighting. On the other hand, the spear had a much longer reach if he needed to keep his distance, but the crossbow was easily better in the range department. The shield was good only if he was going to be on the defensive and that wasn't his style. He knew that with his asthma he had to control the battle, if there was to be one, and end it quickly. Which meant he had to be able to take out his target or targets quickly. And since he had little to no chance with a normal longbow the crossbow was his best option. After strapping on the weapons, he was led out into the arena where to his surprise he was greeted by silence and darkness.

Jack looked around in confusion when he heard the sound of a large fire being lit. At once dozens of torches blazed to life and lit the arena in a dim red glow. In the firelight Jack could barely make out his friends up at the chief's personal box where they had watch Saralia attempt her test. He spotted Saralia and Tiny watching just outside of the arena walls. Just then he spotted movement at the opposite edge of the arena. Six Ibexian guards were carrying a large object covered by a rough cloth. They gently laid the object on the ground and four quickly backed away while the two in front picked up the corners of the cover but did not lift it. The chief then raised his hands and spoke.

"Is the challenger ready?" he asked.

"Can you tell me what I am to do first?" Jack asked in response.

The Chief waved his right arm and the two guards pulled the cover off of the object they had been carrying. At once Jack could see it was a large cage but what was inside is what gave him tremors of fear. It was a creature, nearly thirteen feet in length from nose to tail and mostly covered in dirty white hair. The scaly head reminded him of an alligator, but it had five eyes, two on each side and a solitary one in the middle of its forehead. It had six long, scaly legs and its feet were tipped with razor sharp claws. As soon as it saw its surroundings it started to thrash about trying to break out of its prison. Its bellows echoed around the stone arena.

"Your challenge is to figure out how to defeat this cliff crawler before time runs out or it defeats you." The chief said gesturing to the stone funnel that had been filled with water once more. Jack took a deep breath and readied his crossbow.

"I am ready." Jack shouted over the beast's roars.

The guards pulled on two ropes, one releasing the water from the funnel, and the other to the cage's gate which fell open. Immediately the creature rushed out and started to look around the arena, seemingly trying to find a way to escape. Jack closed one eye and took aim with the crossbow. He looked over the beast trying to figure out just where he should shoot first when he saw it begin to sniff the air. He pulled the trigger and the bolt hit the beast in the neck but to his horror it ricocheted off like it was armor plated. The beast quickly turned towards where the attack had come from and let out a roar. It charged Jack as he was trying to reload his weapon. Just before the creature reached him he fired another bolt this one hitting one of the two left eyes. The creature roared in pain but kept coming and it leapt towards Jack, its claws outstretched ready to tear him into shreds. Before it hit the Ibexian guards thrust their spears out blocking the attack. The beast roared but was quickly cornered and forced back into its cage which was locked behind it.

Jack stood nearby gasping for breath, as the adrenaline coursed through him, he looked at the chief and his friends. The chief frowned and a look of sadness came over him. He raised his hands and addressed the arena.

"The test of intelligence has been failed. The cliff crawler has won. However, the lowlander Tiny will be allowed to hunt the cliff crawler queen and we can all hope that he will succeed where many of our own have failed.

Jack let his head down in defeat and sighed. He thought about what he could have done better when he heard a strange sound coming from the cage. It was a loud chirping sound, and the cliff crawler was the one making it. Suddenly he felt his blood run cold and he quickly loaded another bolt into his weapon.

"Chief you need to evac this area now!" He shouted.

The chief looked down at him in surprise and confusion.

"What do you mean warrior?"

"Get everyone out now!" Jack shouted again. He looked at Stephen who nodded and began to quickly usher their friends out.

Just then he felt the ground shake rhythmically and then he heard the sound of something huge climbing up the arena walls. Just then he heard the cliff crawler chirp again and this time it was answered by a deafening bellow just outside of the wooden room.

"Oh no" he thought. "Mommy's here!"

Chapter 8. Dethrone and Descend.

When the massive creature broke through the wooden ceiling pandemonium broke loose. The spectators started fleeing for their very lives in all directions. Stephen and Victoria quickly tried to get their friends and the Chief out of the arena and out of harm's way. Saralia turned tail and galloped back to where she had left her weapons. And Jack was left alone in the arena watching in horror as the monster crawled down the arena walls and onto the ground in front of him. It was well over seventy feet long from nose to tail. Its head alone was over fifteen feet of teeth and jaws. Jack raised his crossbow but quickly realized that it would be little use against such a creature. He turned and started to run towards an exit but he heard something large whistling towards him. He ducked and slid on the dirt as the monster's massive scaly tail whipped over him and smashed the top of the doorway causing it to collapse. Jack turned around and saw that it was less than ten feet away now. He raised his crossbow again and took aim for one of its five eyes but just before he pulled the trigger, he heard something. The young crawler had started chirping again and then a loud roar came from behind the queen. Jack watched in shock as the large metal cage with the young crawler still inside was hurled into the queen's head.

The impact was so strong it sent the queen staggering to the side. Once it was on its feet again the queen turned to face its new attacker, but Tiny was already rushing towards Jack. Tiny picked up Jack without even slowing down and he barreled through the once blocked door. Once they were out into the cold winter air they were met by the rest of the party and the chief.

"Chief you need to get everyone to safety!" Jack shouted again as Tiny slid to a stop in the snow. Jack jumped out of Tiny's grip and faced the chief. "We'll take care of that monster!"

"But you did not pass the test! Only Tiny can be allowed to fight it according to our customs!" The chief protested. He was met by the sounds of weapons being drawn and bows being strung.

"With all due respect chief, right now the only thing that has a chance of taking that monster down before it destroys your village is us. If you want to argue, fine, we'll have Tiny carry you back to your house where we can discuss the matter of your customs after we have either defeated the beast or all been eaten. It's your choice." Stephen said firmly.

The chief looked at the warriors and then at his personal guards who had just run up to protect their leader. Just then the monster's head broke through the stone walls of the arena. It saw the group and let out a deafening bellow that echoed around the mountains. Shortly thereafter they heard dozens of lesser bellows answering the call and then the cliffsides became alive with movement as nearly a hundred young crawlers staring rushing down them towards the party.

The chief didn't say a word but quickly rushed away with his guards leaving the party alone.

"Alright what's the plan?" Jack asked.

"Tiny get Dani and Annie to safety. The rest of us will try to lure it away." Stephen quickly answered.

Tiny quickly scooped up Annie and Dani and hurried away to the great hall. The rest of the group watched as the queen finally managed to break through the rest of the arena and start lumbering towards them.

"Run!" Victoria screamed.

"To where?" Saralia shouted back.

"Let's get it into a more confined area where it can't turn around." Jack replied.

The three humans climbed onto Saralia's back and she took off as fast as her four legs could carry them. They soon found a narrow street lined with stone houses. There the three humans jumped off and quickly surveyed the soon-to-be battlefield. The houses lining the street were joined together side-by-side with the backs of the houses being set into the mountainsides. They were about two stories tall with two small windows per each floor.

"Ok, I have a plan." Jack shouted as the bellowing of the crawlers drew ever closer. "Tori, and I will take up positions in the houses and try to slow them down. Saralia and Steve you'll act as the bait and keep their attention to you. Tiny should be back within a few minutes. Hopefully we'll have figured out how to kill that thing by then."

The others nodded their agreement and quickly took up their positions. Victoria entered a house of the left side while Jack rushed into one on the right. Just then the crawlers appeared around the corner and as soon as they saw the two warriors in the street they stopped. Stephen drew his sword and readied himself, Saralia dug in her hooves and laid an arrow on her bowstring.

"What are they waiting for?" Stephen asked in bewilderment.

"The queen." Saralia said coldly.

Her assumption proved correct as the massive beast came around the corner and stopped just before the street. Its throat swelled with air before it let out a deafening roar. At once the young crawlers started advancing down the street or some climbing along the outside of the house walls. Jack and Saralia starting shooting at the crawlers as they came closer. Victoria gutted any that came across the windows in front of her. Stephen watched it all as he waited for his turn to strike. Then he noticed something that gave him chills.

"Saralia! The queen isn't coming into the street!" He shouted.

"We need to figure out how to lure her in!" She shouted back. She kept firing arrows into any crawler that got too close. A few arrows found their marks and dropped the crawlers while others glanced off their thick scaly skin and fell short.

Just as the first few reached Stephen and he began to swing his sword and try to cut them down the street echoed with two new sounds that filled the heroes' ears. The first was a high-pitched scream that seemed to stall the crawlers in their tracks emitted by dozens of Ibexian guards who rushed into the fray with their spears at the ready. The second was another deafening roar that matched and surpassed the queen's own bellows as Tiny leaped into the battle. He landed on two crawlers with a crunch and roared again as if he was challenging their leader. The queen bellowed her response and then slowly began to enter the street.

"The One Above! That did the trick!" Saralia shouted over the noise. She then watched as Tiny reached over to his right, grabbed a large door out of its doorframe and used it as a plow as he rushed through the mass of crawlers knocking them aside like toys.

Stephen watched in awe as Tiny continued his attack when an idea came to him. "A trick... Saralia you're a genius!" He shouted before quickly running to the houses on the left. He ran up onto the second story where he found Jack with his left hand in a pocket and his right was loading another bolt into the crossbow. Stephen barely noticed this as he ran to the window and looked down into the chaotic street below.

"What are you doing up here? Jack said in surprise.

"I think I know a way to kill that monster. I've been talking with Tiny about new battle strategies and there's one that could work." Stephen said as he kicked out the window that fell into the street below. He then looked down into the battle and saw Tiny was smashing his way through the crawlers using two he had by the tails in each hand.

"Tiny!" Stephen shouted. He saw the Unkarian pause his attack and look up at the window where he stood. Stephen quickly moved to the back of the room and then sprinted out of the window and jumped towards Tiny. As he flew through the air, he shouted one last command.

"Fastball special!"

Tiny dropped the now dead crawlers, turned around, and cupped his hands together ignoring the crawlers that were now slashing at his feet and legs. Stephen drew his sword as he fell and landed in Tiny's hands. With a grunt Tiny hurled Stephen into the air towards the queen. Stephen held his sword out in front of himself and aimed for the queen's central eye. Stephen landed on its head and plunged his sword into the eye but before he could sink it in deeper the monster roared and reared back while Stephen tried to hold on for his life. After a few seconds the monster landed on its feet and started to shake its head trying to knock Stephen off. Tiny rushed forward, leapt up, and grabbed it by its nose and tried to hold it down.

"Now!" Tiny roared.

Stephen braced himself and drove his sword up to the hilt into the queen's middle eye. After another roar it went limp and crumpled into the street. The young crawlers stopped their attack and looked back at their mother before turning around and rushing away. Stephen pulled his messy sword out of the queen's eye and turned back to face his friends. He then held his sword high in the air and let out a cheer that was quickly echoed by the other warriors and Ibexian guards. After nearly shouting himself hoarse he jumped off of the monster's lifeless body and onto the blood-soaked snow next to Tiny where they were joined by Saralia, Victoria, and Jack.

"That was epic!" Jack shouted giving Stephen a slap on the back.

"Nice move Steve!" Victoria chimed in.

Saralia was about to join in the congratulation giving but Stephen held up a hand to pause as he cleared his throat.

"Sorry, I may have made myself a little hoarse earlier." He wheezed. "No offense Sara."

"Umm, none taken." Saralia replied in confusion.

"Are the others safe?" Jack asked.

The group paused for a moment and then they all heard a crawler bellow followed by a shrill scream in the distance.

"Let's go!" Victoria shouted.

In one motion Saralia grabbed Victoria and swung her onto her back while Tiny grabbed the two men and together, they rushed through the snow towards the great hall.

Once they arrived, they saw to their horror that the crawlers had scratched a hole in the large double doors. Tiny dropped Stephen and Jack in a snowbank and charged at the doors with Saralia and Victoria close behind. Just as Tiny reached the doors he stopped abruptly and Saralia ran into his backside causing Victoria to fly off into the snow.

"What are you doing Tiny?" Saralia sputtered as she pushed past the huge unkarian and into the hall.

Victoria was on her feet in moments and hurried through the doors. When she got inside, she saw the villagers and chieftain huddled at the far end of the room with a barricade of tables between them and the door. By the doorway were over half a dozen crawlers scattered about, a few were still twitching in death but most of them had a single arrow shaft in their central eye. Dani, with an arrow still on her bowstring turned to face the newcomers but lowered her bow when she saw her friends.

"Oh, now you show up with the guards." She said with a mock annoyed tone. "Annie and I had to deal with these things ourselves." Dani swung herself over the makeshift barricade and walked over to her friends.

"Where is Annie?" Victoria asked quickly.

"Here." Annie appeared right next to Victoria wiping crawler blood off her dagger. "Those things are surprisingly easy to kill when you stab them in their middle eyes."

"I told you the weak spots are always the eyes." Dani said as she put the arrow back into her quiver. "Just like those games Jack likes to play. The legend of... something or other."

Stephen and Jack chuckled as they entered the hall with Saralia close behind them.

"Chief I'm afraid you'll have a large mess to clean up." Stephen said.

"The queen has been defeated then?" The chief asked shakily.

"You'll find her carcass along with many other crawlers lying a little way away." Jack said proudly.

The chief's eyes widened as he looked at the victorious party then turning to the other villagers he said. "Quickly! We must begin the harvest and ready a feast for tonight to celebrate the Lowlander's victory!"

The Ibexians rushed out the doors and hurried away while a few stayed behind and began to move the dead crawlers out of the hall.

"Harvest?" Saralia asked confused.

"Cliff crawler meat is a delicacy. To have this much at our doorstep is an opportunity we cannot miss." The chief answered as he left the room.

Jack and Victoria rolled their eyes and Dani groaned.

"You mean the queen was upset because you like eating her young? No wonder it attacked the village." Annie gasped.

"The queen has never come this close to the village before. I am unsure of why she attacked when she did. Now if you will excuse me I have a feast to prepare for you all." The chief replied coldly.

The group watched the chief leave the great hall in disbelief.

"I knew they weren't the brightest folk, but they did bring it on themselves." Stephen said shaking his head.

"Something doesn't add up though." Jack replied. "He said the queen doesn't normally come this close. If the Ibexians hunted and captured the young crawlers but the queen still didn't come into the village, what changed? Why did she come this time?"

"Good question." Victoria replied.

"We should ask the chief about it after the feast is over." Saralia added.

The group nodded their approval and went back to their quarters to clean up from their fight. Jack was just inspecting his crossbow when he heard someone knock at his door.

"Who is it?" he called out.

"It's Steve. Can I come in?" Stephen's voice replied from outside.

Jack jumped up and opened the heavy wooden door and Stephen stepped inside.

"That was some fight back there." Stephen remarked as he sat down on a wooden bench.

"Yeah. That finishing move you did was awesome! I wish I would have thought of that." Jack replied as he returned to cleaning his weapon.

"Jack, can I ask you a question?" Stephen said hesitantly.

"Sure. What's on your mind?" Jack replied putting down the crossbow.

"Jack, you and I have been friends for a long time. We used to keep each other's secrets all the time. I once thought we never kept anything from each other, and I could trust you with anything. But ever since you moved away things changed. We drifted apart and we didn't talk too much anymore. I wish it wasn't like that but there wasn't really anything we could do."

"What are you getting at?"

"When were you going to tell me?"

"Tell you about what?"

"When I came into the room just before Tiny and I pulled the fastball special. I saw you putting something into your pocket. An inhaler."

Jack let out a long sigh and looked down at the stone floor.

"Jack, do you have asthma?"

"Yes. I found out two weeks ago while I was at camp. My parents had set for my mail to be forwarded to me while I was there. I received a letter from the U.S. Army bringing it to my attention. I had suspicions about it, but I wasn't sure until I got the letter. From there I was able to buy an inhaler from the camp nurse."

"Why didn't you mention it earlier? We would have gone easier on you."

"I didn't want you to worry about me. I barely even notice it anyways."

"Except for in the heat of battle or climbing a mountain."

"Yes."

"Do your parents or Dani know?"

"Dani was there when I found out. As for my parents..." Jack sighed again. Stephen leaned closer to his friend.

"When were you going to tell them?"

"I... I don't know how. I was trying to join in the military like my dad and surprise him with the news for his birthday in a few weeks. I used some of his old contacts to get a physical with a recruiter and that's how I found out about the asthma. Now I don't know what to say."

"Just tell them, I'm sure they will understand."

"But my dad... he'll be disappointed in me."

"But you don't have any control over that. I know your dad; he loves you no matter what you will end up doing."

"I know he will always love me. But I want to make him proud of what I have accomplished with my life."

"You're only eighteen. You have a lot of time left to do great things with your life. Is that why you are pushing yourself so hard? Jack even if we manage to become heroes again and save the day how do you expect your dad to believe you when you tell him about this world? I don't want to break your spirit but let's face it, nobody other than those who have been here with us or before us would believe anything about this world."

"Then what am I supposed to do?"

"Talk to your parents when we get back. I know it is hard to live up to a parent's expectations. Look at my dad, he's a big tech genius and currently working on some sort of new holographic watch. While I do like to tinker with machines, I'm no computer genius. Never have, probably never will be. But I know that even if I don't make my Dad proud in the field he has mastered I know his love is greater than that and no matter what I do with my life he will love me and be proud of me for who I am in God. That's what matters most to him and myself, and nothing will change that."

Jack looked up at his friend, his eyes beginning to water and nodded. Stephen didn't say another word but embraced his friend for a few seconds before letting him go. The two men than sat quietly and talked for nearly an hour before they were called to the feast.

The feast was a lavish affair with the victorious party being seated with the chief and his family. When they were served the crawler meat even Dani admitted it was better than anything she had eaten on earth. Just as they were finishing dinner an Ibexian messenger rushed in and pulled the chief away.

"What is that all about?" Victoria asked.

"No idea but it must be something big to pull the chief away like that." Stephen replied.

Annie winked at her friends and then abruptly disappeared. After nearly ten minutes she appeared back in her chair as if she had never left.

"The messenger was there to tell the chief that somebody has stolen a 'blade of embers' from its mountain shrine." Annie told the group in a whisper.

"Blade of Embers?" Jack asked.

"Must be some special weapon." Stephen answered.

"In this world there are ancient weapons that have some sort of power that resides in them. Only those who are chosen can actually wield them, if you are not the chosen wielder, you'll get a nasty shock if you touch them." Victoria explained.

"The weapons are extremely tough, and the weapons also grant enhanced strength and stamina to the wielder. However, some weapons have their own unique powers too. I had one known as 'The Servant's Sword' that little blade could cut through almost anything." Stephen added.

"If that weapon was so good, why don't you have it now?" Dani asked.

"Because Groman has it now. He was chosen to bear The Empty Sword and we learned that it needed to have the servant's sword inserted into it to fill its full potential." Annie answered.

"Don't forget he had to be wearing my broken gauntlets too." Victoria chimed in.

"That's interesting." Jack said. "Do you think we may have some chosen weapon as well?"

"Those weapons are very few and far between. The odds of finding one are very slim and when you add to that the chances of it being chosen for you it is highly unlikely." Saralia replied.

"Are the special items only weapons or are there other tools as well?" Dani asked.

"I have no idea." Stephen answered.

After their discussion the party saw that the feast was beginning to die down, so they made their way back to their own quarters for their last night on the mountain.

The next morning the party were assembled in the village square and preparing to depart when the chief arrived.

"Are you ready to begin your descent?" He asked.

"Yes sir. No offense but I am ready to be back in a warmer environment." Jack said.

"Here here!" Saralia echoed. "If we stay much longer, I may start growing my winter coat early!"

The chief chuckled. "Very well adventurers. You have my blessing to return to your journey. I know you will find the man whom you seek."

"Thank you, sir." Annie said quietly.

"And if you happen to find a unique black sword with a cracked red blade. Do what you can to bring it back. Someone stole it from its shrine last night while you were in battle. It is a priceless artifact we must have back." The chief added.

"We will do what we can sir!" Stephen said.

With that the party began their journey through the village to the north and then down the long twisting pathway on the side of the mountain. After about half an hour they spotted a large cave with piles of bones lying about frozen to the ground.

"That must be the crawler's cave." Victoria said quietly.

"Think they know we're here?" Stephen asked.

Tiny turned and walked over to the mouth of the cave and let out a deafening roar that echoed all around them and seemed to go all the way through the cave. When nothing was heard afterwards Tiny shrugged and rejoined his companions.

"Tiny scare little lizards off." He said.

"Yes, you did." Dani replied with a giggle.

Just then a chirping noise was heard, and the group reached for their weapons when Annie held up her right arm.

"I cannot believe it! He found me!" She squealed in delight as the little red flying lizard appeared in the skies above. Annie whistled and the lizard dove for her outstretched arm and quickly ran up her sleeve. "Poor little flyer, he is chilled to the bone." Annie said softly as she reached into her sleeve with her left arm and pulled out a rolled-up piece of parchment paper. She unrolled it and read the message to the party.

My dearest Annalio

I have sent your flizard to you so you may have a way of contacting us if you are in desperate need of help. However, it would take us a while to reach you, so I am afraid you and your friends are on your own. Do not worry, The One Above is watching over you all and your brother. He will bring you back safely and I know that you will return to Areiop one day.

With regards.

Windmere.

"Mother always knew what I needed before I ever did." Saralia said quietly.

"At least we have a way of contact if we need it." Stephen said.

"Just not right away. I have to warm little flyer up before we can send him out again." Annie replied.

The group nodded and continued their descent. After several hours of uneventful climbing down the wide path they spotted the tops of trees in the distance.

"Look we're almost at the bottom!" Dani shouted in excitement.

After another hour of walking the adventurers found themselves in something that they had not really expected.

"A swamp?" Jack asked in surprise.

"This world doesn't always follow the same rules as ours Jack." Stephen replied. He looked around at their surroundings. There were trees dotted all around them but thankfully they weren't as think as the kittrian woods. The ground was soft and muddy but took their weight. A few ponds and streams were also dotted around the area as well.

"So we press onwards then?" Saralia asked.

"Yes. We must be getting close to where Groman was taken. I can feel it!" Annie shouted as she started to make her way through a rough, muddy path. The rest of the party deposited their winter cloaks in Saralia's saddlebags and after thanking her for carrying the load followed behind her.

As they made their way through the bog Saralia's voice broke the silence.

"Stop! Did you feel that?" She asked worriedly.

"Feel what?" Victoria asked.

"I felt the ground vibrating like something big was nearby." Saralia replied turning about and quickly looking around as if to see something.

"There's nothing there." Dani said. She lifted the hem of her dress to keep it out of the mud and continued on. The rest of the part followed with Saralia nervously bringing up the rear.

After a little while Annie slowed her pace so she was next to Victoria.

"I do not want to sound paranoid, but do you feel like someone is watching us?" She whispered.

"Now that you mention it. I have been getting that feeling too. Have you seen anything or anyone yet?" Victoria quietly replied.

"No. But I will keep looking around."

"I think this marsh is giving everyone the creeps."

Soon after crossing a quiet stream, they came to a large area of dry grassy ground surrounded by trees. Stephen looked up at the sun as it began its trek lower towards the east.

"Here's as good a spot as any to make camp." He said.

The others agreed and began unrolling their sleeping mats while Saralia stood nearby, her tail swishing nervously.

"Saralia don't worry. We haven't seen any sign of a threat so far. If you're that worried you can take the first watch tonight." Jack said.

"I cannot shake the feeling that there is something big nearby. I can feel the vibrations in the ground through my hooves." Saralia replied.

"Are you sure it's not just Tiny's footsteps?" Dani chuckled.

Saralia gave Dani a quick glare before walking a short distance away. "I know the feeling of everybody's footsteps. It certainly is not Tiny..."

Saralia's voice was cut off as a mountain of mud and earth erupted in between her and her friends. She let out a scream almost like a horse and tried to run but the monster was already on top of her.

"Sara!" Victoria screamed.

Chapter 9. The Flitnao Fighters.

"What on earth is that thing?" Jack shouted as he loaded his weapon.

"No idea, just scare it off or kill it!" Stephen replied as he drew his sword and raised his shield.

"We need to draw it away from Sara!" Victoria said.

Stephen started banging his sword against his shield and watched as the monster turned to face him. It was nearly twelve feet tall and seemed to be one huge mouth with rows of teeth all around it in a spiral formation. On the top of its mouth was a small cluster of eyes with two facing its front, two on the sides, and two at the rear. Its body was lined with dozens of legs like a millipede which were slowly trying to pull itself back into the ground. Around its mouth were four long mandibles with crab-like claws and they had Saralia in their grip as they lifted her into the air and towards its mouth.

"Cut the mandibles off!" Stephen shouted as he rushed the beast and started hacking away at a lower claw. He saw to his horror his sword just glanced off the thick exoskeleton and barely left a mark. Jack and Victoria tried their own blades and achieved similar results.

"Tiny don't let her get eaten!" Dani screamed.

Tiny rushed forwards and grabbed onto the struggling Saralia and pulled with all his might. The monster let out a loud hiss and continued its retreat into the ground.

Dani started shooting it with arrows but while they easily penetrated its slimy hide they seemed to have no effect on the massive creature as it was just too big to notice.

"Can you aim for its eyes?" Annie shouted.

Jack loaded his crossbow and tried to back up in order to get a clear shot but tripped over a root and fell on his behind in the mud.

"I'm on it!" Victoria said. She quickly used her tekko kagi claws to climb her way up the monster's side and towards its head. The beast tried to shake her off but she dug her claws in deeper and held on. Once she was close enough, she started slashing away at the unprotected eyes, the monster's black blood spraying everywhere. She kept going and dug her claws in as deep as she could. The monster let out another hiss and stopped moving, releasing Saralia from its grip only a few inches from its gaping maw. Saralia and Tiny tumbled to the ground and Victoria slid down the worm's side into the marshy ground with a splat.

"Good idea going for the eyes." Victoria panted.

"How did you know to go for them?" Jack asked as he tried to wipe the mud from his clothes.

"Well, it was the same weakness as the crawlers..." Annie began.

"And?" Dani prodded.

"A voice told me." Annie finished.

"A voice?" Stephen questioned.

"I do not know who it was or where it came from. I just heard someone say to hit the eyes." Annie replied.

"Tiny heard it too. Tiny think voice came from tree over there." Tiny added.

The group looked at the tree that Tiny had referred to. It seemed to be a simple marsh tree if it not for it being on the bigger side it wouldn't really stand out much more than any of the others.

Just then Saralia began to panic again.

"The One Above! There are more coming! I can feel them!" she screamed.

"To arms!" Stephen shouted as dozens of smaller worms began to burst out of the ground surrounding the party.

"Dani! Fire at will!" Jack shouted as he fired a bolt from his crossbow into a worm's eye causing it to drop to the ground.

"Form a circle with our backs to each other!" Stephen shouted. The party formed a circle and began slashing at any worms who came too close. Soon it was only chaos as more and more worms began to come out of the ground and attack. Stephen and Victoria were slashing away with their blades. Saralia was using her swords and stomping worms with her hooves. Tiny was pulling the worms out of the ground with his bare hands and squashing them in his fists like one would squish a tomato. Jack and Dani were shooting as fast as they could reload their weapons and in the middle of it all was Annie who was desperately trying to stay out of harm's way.

"We can't hold them off forever! There's just no end to these guys!" Stephen shouted. Just then a new voice broke through the sounds of battle.

"Flitnao fighters! To battle!"

Suddenly the air became filled with miniature, winged warriors zipping from worm-to-worm slashing with their weapons and firing their small longbows.

Dani tried to get a closer look at their new allies and saw that they were no more than ten inches high. Their skin tone varied from very pale green to white, their hair following suit with their long, pointed ears poking through it. They had four long gossamer wings like a dragonfly protruding from their backs. They were dressed in what seemed to be clothes and armor made from plants and tree bark and their weapons were nearly as big as they were. They seemed to be quite agile in the air as they attacked the worms from nearly every angle, darting in and out like mosquitos, slashing and stabbing as they went.

"Watch out!" A voice called out, interrupting Dani's thoughts. One of the tiny warriors zipped past her waving a large rapier. It darted around her and attacked a worm that had come up out of the ground behind her. The warrior zipped around the worm stabbing and slashing as it went until it went limp. The small warrior then turned to face Dani and she could get a better look at their unexpected allies. She could see it was very similar to a female human but still around ten inches in height. Her skin was a very pale grey, and her hair which was tied in a long braid that went past her waist was as white as snow. Except for long pointed ears that stuck out through her hair her face was very much like a human's, with a rounded chin, and piercing jade green eyes. She was dressed in a green tunic and trousers with brown boots with a breastplate, arm guards, and shin guards made of something like birch bark. Her four long gossamer wings had green scales on the tips and where they attached to her back. The rapier she held in her right hand was a single pointed blade nearly twelve inches long and it had a cup hilt made out of a light pink metal fashioned in the shape of a flower protecting her hand.

"You need to keep focused on the battle at hand young one!" The little warrior called out before dashing off to attack another worm. Dani looked after her new ally and joined the fight once more.

Soon all of the worms were either lying dead on the ground or retreating to their burrows. The group began to relax as they watched the tiny fighters begin to group around them.

"The battle is won young warriors!" one of the small warriors called out.

"Indeed, it is!" Stephen called back.

"We have you to thank for that. If you had not arrived when you did, we may not have survived." Annie added.

"The thanks are not needed. That mother worm has been a thorn in our sides for far too long. Our small weapons were useless against it." The warrior replied as he flew forward towards the group. He had a dark olive colored skin with dark brown hair that was cleanly cut like a soldier's. He was dressed in a black-hooded tunic and trousers with a breastplate and arm guards the color of ebony wood. His face seemed rough with a pointed nose and chin with fiery red eyes to match. His wings had red scaled edges and tips. He wielded a one-handed sword nearly thirteen inches in length with an ornate vine engraving running down the blade.

"Were you watching us the whole time?" Jack asked.

"Aye lad. We knew about your arrival ever since you came down from the mountains. We are not accustomed to visitors and were wanting to see if you were friend or foe." The warrior then drew his sword and held it with its tip pointing towards the ground lowering his head with the other fighters following suit. "My name is Urano and we the flitnao people are in your debt for killing the mother worm. I swear upon my honor as the leader of the flitnao fighters if we can be of service to you in any way you need only to ask."

"Thank you Urano. You are too kind." Annie replied with a smile.

"Do you know of a good place where we can make camp for the night?" Stephen asked. "The worms kinda destroyed this area with their holes."

"Say no more! You will all be honored guests in our fair city of Messingar!" Urano shouted. "Follow my warriors and myself and we will lead you there!" He then turned around and flew away with his warriors quickly falling into a "V" formation behind him. Stephen took the lead as the rest of the group started their trek through the marsh once more wading through the mud and algae covered pools. Suddenly a loud noise like a shriek mixed with a horse's whinny rang out through the swamp followed by a loud splash. The group turned around to see Saralia, who had been bringing up the rear, had slipped on the mud and fallen into a deep pool. She tried to stand up again and let out a gasp of shock when she saw the green algae had clung to her tan flanks and turned them a shade of green.

"No no no!" This cannot be happening!" She shouted before stepping onto the banks only to sink up to knees in mud. She groaned again and hung her head in defeat.

Stephen started to laugh but stopped himself when he saw Victoria was about to punch him. Some of the flitnao were not so polite however and many of them began to laugh uncontrollably.

Tiny rushed over and quickly pulled Saralia free. She looked herself over and dejectedly resumed her slow pace at the back of the line. Dani and Annie did their best to guide her to prevent more mishaps all the while some of flitnao continued to snicker and chuckle about their new friend's misfortune.

Just as the sun finally set behind the trees, they all came around a bend and found themselves in a large grove of soft grass and wildflowers surrounded by towering trees that formed a natural barrier between the grove and the swamp. The flitnao flew to the largest of the trees and either landed on its many limbs or hovered nearby. Urano hovered in the center of the grove and waited for the group to all arrive inside. Once they were there he held up his hands and shouted.

"These heroes slew the mother worm in battle this night! They are to be our honored guests at our celebration feast!"

As soon as he finished the grove was lit up by hundreds of small colorful lanterns made out of flower petals and leaves and strange vines the glowed a soft green. More and more flitnao people appeared from their hiding places in the trees and came over to inspect their new friends. Soon nearly the whole party was enjoying a feast of roasted meat, fruits, and vegetables all harvested from the swamp.

Dani was enjoying a bite of something that reminded her of a pear when she looked to her right and saw Saralia quietly lying down at the foot of one of the large trees looking rather dejectedly at her mud and algae covered hooves and flanks.

"She is not accustomed to traversing a swamp, is she?" A voice said.

Dani looked to her left and saw the female flitnao from before. She had changed from her green attire and armor into a long red dress that seemed to be made from rose petals. Dani sighed and nodded.

"She hasn't had a very fun trip so far. It seems like we haven't been many places someone like her is meant for. I think she really wants to help but feels like she is only slowing us down."

The flitnao woman flew over to Dani and sat down on her shoulder.

"I know how that can feel sometimes."

"What do you mean? You saved me from that worm back there. I don't think you were slowing anyone down at all!"

"What is your name child?"

"Dani"

"Well Dani among the flitnao people there are some of us who have a special gift. Sometimes we can see what is about to happen before it happens. It is not a common gift, and it takes a very long time to master."

"You have that gift?"

"Yes. But as I have not trained it very much the visions and images are very blurry, and I have trouble making out what they mean. But my friends and fellow warriors, especially Urano always try to depend on me to how a battle is going to go before we even attack. But because I have not been trained very much, I cannot tell them much. So, we are forced to wait until I, or someone else, get a clearer vision. So instead of being able to help my lack of clear vision only slows the fighters down."

"I can see why you think that but honestly I think you all did very well back there vision or no vision."

The little woman sighed. "Perhaps. But what matters now is finding a way to help your friend there."

"Do you have an idea?"

"It may not be much, but I can have some of the other women try to help clean her up a little. I do not know much about her but cleaning up after a battle usually helps me feel better."

"I think she would appreciate that. Thank you." Dani said with a smile. The little woman's wings buzzed as she took off again.

"Wait!" Dani called out. "What was your name again?"

The flitnao smiled. "My name is Monaria."

"Nice to meet you Monaria. And thank you."

"It is my pleasure to help wherever I can."

As Monaria flew away to see to Saralia, Stephen, Jack, Victoria and Urano were talking around a small campfire.

"So, I must ask you, what brings strangers like you into our home?" Urano asked.

"A friend of ours was kidnapped from the lands past the mountains to the south nearly two weeks ago." Jack replied.

Urano rubbed his chin thoughtfully. "We did hear a lot of commotion in the skies above us during the night around that time. We were uncertain who or what it was and did not venture out to help. However, a large object fell from the sky that night and landed in the swamp a few miles north of here. I sent some of my best scouts to investigate it, but the worms have been usually active in that area."

"Can't you just fly over them?" Victoria asked.

"One would think so, but they are not the only predators in this area. Some are far worse than the worms..."

"What kind of object was it? Did any of the scouts get close enough to see it?" Stephen asked.

"The only scout who saw it from a distance said it was some type of sword. And the worms were swarming all around it like they were guarding it." Urano replied.

"Can we go see it tonight?" Annie chimed in.

"I am afraid not young one. We do not leave our grove after dark. To do so would be suicidal for us." Urano said.

"What about me?" Annie replied. "Especially when I can do this." She promptly vanished from sight. Urano blinked several times but held his composure.

"That is a fine trick. However, the worms do not rely on their sight to hunt. Rather they can smell you and feel your footsteps. I imagine your two larger companions are the reason the mother attacked you. She only comes out after the biggest prey she can find. Besides that, there are other predators that roam the swamps at night. The eagle bats are quite agile in the air and many a flitnao has been lost while trying to find their way home in the dark. No, we will wait until first light to venture out and get a better look at that sword. Perhaps with the defeat of the mother the worms will be less inclined to attack us."

"So, if the swamp is so dangerous why stay here at all?" Victoria asked.

"This is the only life many of us have known. I was only a youngling when our forefathers discovered this sanctuary. And we have been living here for several generations. All we need we can find here among the reeds and trees. This grove is a natural barrier against all those creatures who would do us harm.

"Several generations? If you don't mind my asking sir. How old are you?" Stephen questioned.

Urano gave a wry smile before continuing. "Three hundred and twenty-six. And I am barely half the age of our oldest elders. We have found that the roots and branches have grown together so thickly that nothing can penetrate them and the opening you and your friends entered through is always under heavy guard." Urano replied. "Now if you will excuse me, I will retire to bed. I would advise you all to do the same, we must have our strength up for our journey tomorrow."

The three humans and kittrian stood there in silence while they let what they had just heard. Victoria broke the silence with a loud yawn.

"I am going to take his advice and turn in. I will see you all in the morning." She said before walking over to where she had left her bedroll. She noticed Saralia lying nearby telling the tale of how she and Victoria had rescued Annie months ago to a small group of flitnao women who were happily buzzing about trying to clean the last bits of mud off her hooves. Victoria couldn't help but let out a soft chuckle, she could easily tell Saralia was stretching the story to make herself sound more heroic, but she was too tired to interject. Instead, she laid down and was almost asleep when a familiar voice spoke in her ear.

"Tori, are you asleep?" Annie's voice came out of thin air.

Victoria rolled over to face Annie, but she couldn't see her. She propped herself up with her right elbow and looked around.

"I was, but I can talk. What's wrong Annie?"

"What do you think we will find tomorrow?"

"The big sword that Urano had mentioned."

"Do... do you think... its Groman's sword?"

Victoria paused for a moment. She hadn't really thought of it. She just figured that since the flitnao were so small that any average sword would be large to them.

"I don't know Annie. What do you think?"

Annie reappeared kneeling next to Victoria's bedroll, Victoria quickly saw why had had chosen to remain invisible, Annie was crying.

"I cannot get the thought out of my mind that it is the Empty sword, and we are going to find..." She broke down into tears again and Victoria quickly sat up and pulled her in for a hug.

"I don't know what we will find tomorrow. But I do know that we can, and we will make it through whatever comes together. We will not give up until we find your brother. Groman is a tough man now. Even if he lost his sword somehow, I know he would not stop until he came back to you."

Annie sniffed and wiped the tears from her eyes.

"Thank you, Tori."

Annie then laid down next to Victoria and was soon asleep on the soft grass. Victoria laid back down and was soon asleep herself. However high above them Monaria sat, perched on a tree branch watching the goings on below.

"You will not find him young one. He will find you." She whispered before flying into a hole in the tree and into her own little bed.

Chapter 10. Fallen weapons.

That night while everyone else was asleep Stephen lay awake in his bedroll. He rolled over on his left side trying to find a more comfortable position when he heard Victoria sigh softly.

"Tori?" He whispered. He heard her move around under her blanket, but she didn't speak. "Can't sleep either eh?"

Victoria sighed again. "I can't get something Annie said earlier out of my mind."

"Oh? What's that?"

"She thinks the sword that fell from the sky is The Empty Sword."

"Well it would make sense as Groman was carried off by flying..."

Victoria shushed him quickly.

"That's why I can't get it out of my mind. What if it is?"

Stephen lay silently for a few minutes contemplating the problem.

"I guess we will have to choose to either continue on or return back to Areiop. Even if we find his sword it doesn't mean he's dead."

"I know. But he really wasn't much of a fighter while we were here last time. It was only after Annie was injured, he really started to train."

"And who trained him in martial arts?"

Victoria sighed again. "Me."

"And how good are you in said martial arts?"

"Second degree blackbelt and two second place finishes at the state tournaments."

"Also, he still has the broken gauntlets meaning he's far from defenseless even without his sword."

"But still, what we do, or say if we find it? Annie will be heartbroken for sure."

"I don't know. Just think and pray about it. I'm sure one of us will have an answer for her when the time comes."

"You're right. I guess I haven't thought of that yet."

"They may call God a different name over here, but He is still God wherever we go."

"If I ascend into heaven you are there, if I descend into hell you are there." Victoria quoted.

"He knows what is going on. Especially since we don't."

"I know. It's just easy to forget sometimes."

The twins lay there silently for a few minutes before Stephen's voice broke the still night.

"We should try to get a little sleep tonight. We need to be ready for whatever we find tomorrow."

Both twins lay in their bedrolls and closed their eyes before saying a quick prayer asking for protection for themselves and Groman and for wisdom in how to handle whatever they might find in the morning.

That next morning the group was awoken by the smell of eggs and vegetables being cooked up for breakfast.

"Good morning fellow warriors!" Urano called out to them as he flew by. He was dressed in a royal blue tunic with brown trousers, his dark ebony armor and his sword in its scabbard hanging at his side. "Once you have eaten my soldiers and I will escort you to the sword from the sky. We should arrive there by midday as long as we don't meet up with any..." He was interrupted by a low mumble below him.

"Tiny smell food..." Tiny said. He slowly sat up and rubbed his eyes.

"Indeed, you do my giant friend." Urano chuckled. "Breakfast is being served on the north side of the clearing, please help yourself."

Tiny stood up and lumbered over to where a team of flitnao were busily stirring a large pot of what looked like oatmeal and cooking some meat and mushrooms over a large fire. Urano turned back to look at the rest of the party.

"As I was saying as long as we do not run into too many monsters we should arrive at the sword by midday."

"Understood." Jack replied.

"Now let's eat!" Dani chimed in.

While they did enjoy their breakfast Victoria and Stephen couldn't help but notice Annie was quieter than normal during the meal. Dani tried to get her to join in a conversation or two, but Annie really wasn't in a talking mood. Victoria worried that if her suspicions were true her demeanor would quickly plummet, and they may have to carry her home.

Shortly after breakfast the group gathered their things and prepared to move out of the grove. As they readied themselves Dani looked around at the trees surrounding them. Most were like huge oak trees with long twisted branches that almost seemed to intertwine with each other like a barrier Urano had mentioned. Also dotted about on the tree trunks she spotted little doorways and a few little porches that indicated a flitnao home. Some of them even had laundry hanging out to dry while others had various weapons like swords, rapiers, and javelins hanging around them, so they were ready for use at a moment's notice.

"Since we are so small, we have to be ready for anything." A familiar voice spoke by Dani's left shoulder. She turned and saw Monaria wearing a red tunic and brown trousers and boots with her armor and rapier hanging at her side.

"That makes sense. Jack is always talking about being prepared for all occasions." Dani replied.

"Even though some of us can see the future it is always good to be ready."

"Are you coming with us to find the sword?"

"As one of Urano's top lieutenants I would hardly think of missing it. Besides I have had a vision that I need to stay with you and your group."

"Did you vision tell you why you think you should stay with us or what will happen?"

Monaria sighed and began to hover downwards towards the ground. Dani held out her hand to catch her. Monaria landed on the palm of her hand and stood there with a somber face and her wings drooping.

"I told you that I need more training to be sure. I cannot tell you what I have seen as I do not know what it was to begin with."

"Right, I'm sorry Monaria. I didn't mean to upset you." Dani said quietly.

Monaria looked at Dani and took flight again. "It is alright. Maybe with time I will be able to better use my gift like the others."

"I hope so." Dani replied.

Soon the party and a small contingent of flitnao fighters were departing the safety of the grove and slowly making their way through the swamp. Urano and most of his fighters flew ahead while Monaria and two other fighters stayed with the rest of the adventurers. The group mostly talked among themselves as they walked, sometimes stopping when Urano or his scouts warned them of large pools of water or quicksand they had to avoid.

After several hours of traveling Stephen was passing a large clump of bushes when he spotted a glint of something golden hidden inside. He quietly stopped walking and waited for the others to press on before investigating. Once he was quite sure nobody else could see him, he quickly pulled the bushes apart to see what was reflecting the light. Once he saw what it was, he felt his heart sink into his legs. It was a large leather scabbard and sword belt, ornately decorated with gold patterns on its sides. It was Groman's scabbard, the same one he used to house the Empty Sword. He quietly picked it up and strapped it in place on his back under his shield, so it wasn't easily noticeable. Just as he tightened the belt in place, he heard someone shout.

"For the glory of the flitnao!"

He drew his own sword and rushed to where he heard the shout come from. Before he reached them, he heard a loud chorus of screeches that were quickly drowned out by a deafening roar from Tiny that shook the trees around him. Stephen quickened his pace and saw the group standing around with their weapons at the ready. The flitnao were flying about as if they were checking for any more enemies. That's when Stephen noticed the large creatures lying on the ground. They were bat-like creatures, larger than an eagle, with sharp teeth and large claws on their feet.

"What happened?" He gasped as he rejoined his friends.

"And where were you a moment ago?" Victoria asked.

"I had a rock in my boot. Sorry I missed all the fun." Stephen quipped.

"Aye lad, it was a worthy battle to start my morning!" Urano laughed as he sheathed his sword.

"Those... things came out of nowhere!" Dani shivered.

"That is why we do not go out after dark. These must have just been getting to their roosts when we came by." Monaria said as she put her rapier back in its place on her hip.

"Well my friends we are nearly to where my scouts reported seeing the sword from the sky. Shall we venture on?" Urano asked.

"Let's go." Jack replied.

The group started to move on, but Stephen quietly put a hand on Victoria's shoulder and pulled her back.

"What gives?" She asked in surprise.

Stephen said nothing but turned around and pulled his shield down revealing the empty scabbard. Victoria gasped and held her hand to her mouth.

"So, we know what is waiting for us don't we?" She whispered sadly.

"Yes." Stephen replied.

"What are we going to do?"

"I don't know but we had better think of something fast before..." Stephen was cut off by a loud wail from further ahead. The twins hurried over to what they had dreaded they would find.

When they arrived at the scene, they had to stop to take it all in. They had arrived at the edge of a small clearing covered with grass and wildflowers with the late morning sun streaming through the trees. Saralia and Tiny were nearby in the shadows of the trees looking on. Jack and the flitnao were just beside them and in the center of the clearing Dani was bending over Annie who had fallen on her knees in the soft grass. Annie was crying and Dani was trying to comfort her all the while looking at what had caused her to break down. Just in front of the two girls was a large ornate sword with its hilt sticking out of the earth. Almost as if someone had purposely driven it into the ground.

Victoria felt tears begin to well up in her own eyes as she quietly walked over to Annie and knelt down beside her. Dani stepped back and joined Jack and the flitnao fighter who stood by somberly.

"I was right... We have lost him." Annie sobbed quietly.

"I... I don't know." Victoria replied quietly.

"What are we going to do now?" Dani asked.

"I don't know." Stephen replied.

"Maybe we should not keep going, maybe we should go back home." Annie said as she stood up and began to walk away.

"Just because we found the empty sword doesn't mean Groman is gone." Stephen said quietly.

"I will send out all of my scouts to search every inch of this swamp until your brother is found if that will ease your pain young one." Urano said.

Annie turned towards the flitnao leader when someone else's voice caught her attention.

"No... Not dead... but not safe... to the east we must go...." Monaria said hesitantly. She hovered in place for a few seconds like she was in a trance before passing out and falling. Victoria lunged forward and managed to catch her in her hands before she landed on a rock. As she stood back up, Monaria began to stir in her hands for a second before sitting up and looking around.

"Why are you all looking at me like that?" she asked puzzled.

"You don't remember what you just said?" Jack asked in surprise.

"No. The last thing I remember was seeing the sword there in the dirt." She replied.

"You said my brother was not dead, then something else and finally something about going east." Annie quickly added.

"She said that Groman wasn't dead but that he also wasn't safe." Stephen chimed in.

"I must have had a vision then." Monaria whispered as she took flight again. "I noticed I can lose control when I have them and not remember what I said. The elders say it is because I have not been able to train my mind enough."

"Well, we heard all that we needed to hear. We must head east right now!" Annie shouted.

"Aye, that you should. And I shall join you on your adventure!" Urano shouted drawing his sword and giving it an exaggerated swing towards the east. "My fighters shall return to Messingar to protect it until my return."

"And I will join you as well." Monaria added. "It would seem that I am destined to be with you for this journey."

"Alright then. Let's move out!" Jack shouted before rushing off in a different direction. The rest of the group watched for a few seconds before Stephen spoke up.

"Jack wait!"

Jack stopped and turned around.

"Wait? Your friend is in danger, and you want me to wait?" Jack replied quickly.

"The sun rises and sets the opposite way to our world. You're going west..." Victoria said quietly. Dani and Annie giggled as Jack turned a faint shade of red as he walked back to the group.

"We should try to bring the sword with us. I do not think it is right to just leave it here." Annie said quietly.

"I agree." Jack replied as he stepped over and tried to grasp the hilt only to leap back in surprise. "Ow! What was that?" He cried out in pain.

"I told you that the empty sword is among the ancient weapons, only those destined to wield it can touch it without being hurt." Victoria replied.

"Right, let's see if..." Stephen said as he walked over, grasped the hilt and pulled it from its resting place in the dirt. "I'm still worthy." He said with a smirk. He sheathed it in its scabbard strapped to his back and looked at the group who were giving him quizzical glances. "My previous sword is a part of this sword. Groman let me hold it last time I was here so I knew it would work."

"Now that we have that settled let us go!" Saralia said as she took off at a trot with the rest of the group doing their best to keep up with her.

Soon they noticed the swamp giving way to a thick forest full of very tall trees that seemed like cedar trees but had very large leaves like an oak tree. The ground became firmer and there were large nuts the size of softballs dotting the ground. But there was one thing that everyone quickly noticed.

"It's too quiet and still." Dani commented quietly.

"Where are the bird songs? The chattering of nutsnatchers? And the whistle of the wind in the trees?" Saralia added.

"I've got a bad feeling about this." Jack said.

"Something very bad happened here." Monaria said.

"Did you see anything about this?" Victoria asked.

"No, but the quietness of this forest is almost as if it saw some horrible act and is now in the act of mourning." Monaria replied.

"I suggest we have our weapons at the ready, my fellow adventurers." Urano added.

Stephen, Victoria, Monaria, Urano and Annie drew their blades while Jack loaded his crossbow. Saralia and Dani strung their bows and Tiny picked up a fallen tree as a club. Once they were ready the group slowly marched on. After another half hour of walking Saralia and Jack who were both in the lead stopped abruptly. Jack held up a fist and took a knee. The group stopped quickly and crouched down as best they could.

"There's someone behind that tree." Jack hissed quietly.

They all looked and sure enough they could just barely make out the form of a winged figure standing behind a large tree about sixty feet away.

"We shall investigate." Urano said as he and Monaria quickly flew towards the stranger. Once they got close they split up and flew around the tree one on each side. The group heard a loud gasp from Monaria and they quickly rushed to where their small friends were.

"What is it?" Stephen gasped as he came around the tree. He stopped short and stared at what he saw.

It was a strange figure, almost like the Blakmians he had come to know on his first visit. It was just short of six feet tall. It had a rounded human-like face with a pointed nose and large eyes. It had very dark brown hair that gave way into similarly colored feathers that covered most of its body that could be seen under its brown tunic and breeches. Its hands and feet were taloned like a bird of prey's and covered in bird-like scales up to the elbows on the arms and to the backwards bending knees on its legs. It had two huge wings covered in dark brown feathers that drooped on the ground behind it. There were two ornate daggers lying at its feet and two more tucked into its tunic. However, it was not any of this that had caused the group so much surprise. It was the two arrow shafts sticking out of its chest pinning it to the tree trunk.

"What kind of being is this?" Jack asked.

"It looks like a Blackmian, like Peregrine." Victoria replied.

"I'd agree but there are some differences." Stephen added. "The wings are smaller, wider, and more curved. The face is more round and the eyes are much bigger."

Annie, who had stayed back ventured forwards and looked at the dead warrior. She let out a gasp and jumped back.

"Annie what's wrong?" Dani asked.

"That... that thing is just like the creatures who attacked Areiop and carried Groman away!" Annie replied shakily.

"Are you sure?" Saralia asked.

"I... I do not know. I did not get a very good look at them when they attacked. I mostly saw a shadow of one when I was trying to contact Tori through the pendant."

"So that's why you screamed." Victoria said quietly.

"I don't blame you. Seeing one these things at night would scare me too." Dani said giving Annie a quick hug.

Stephen turned his attention from the dead warrior and noticed Tiny had walked up a nearby hill to the east and stopped near the top.

"What do you see Tiny?" He called out.

"Not good things. More dead." Tiny replied coldly.

The rest of the group slowly joined their friend at the top of the tree covered hill. What they saw sent chills down their spines. It was the remains of a fierce battle with hundreds of dead warriors like the one they had found lying about on the ground or even hanging from tree branches. Broken weapons and arrows lay around on the ground and stuck into trees and bodies. Dani and Annie covered their mouths with their hands stifling a gasp. Victoria felt sick to her stomach while the rest of the group looked on with a blank expression.

Jack was the first to move down the hill and among the bodies. He examined one closely and turned back to the group.

"This battle happened recently. I'd say within six hours. They're stiff but not quite odorous yet." He called out.

"Who attacked them?" Victoria asked.

"That's the thing. I can't tell who won or lost. I only see the defeated." Jack replied. "If I had to guess I'd say they were fighting each other."

The group then ventured down the hill and began to look around. Stephen walked over to one particularly large warrior who lay slumped against a boulder. He saw its eyes were still open in a look that seemed like surprise. He gently reached out his hand and closed them in respect. He then looked closer and saw that there were no cuts or marks made by a blade or arrow. The only damage he could see was a purple bruise on its face and its chest seemed to have been caved in slightly as if something big or powerful had hit it.

"Hey Jack, come here for a sec." He called out. Jack looked up and tossed aside a short sword he had been examining and walked over.

"What's up?" Jack asked.

"Look at this one. I don't see any marks from a blade or arrow." Stephen replied.

Jack looked closer for a second before gently pushing against its chest with his right hand.

"Ribs are broken. Feels like internal bleeding too. Something really strong must have punched him." Jack remarked.

"Yeah that's what I thought. The only thing is I don't think any of those warriors could have done something like this."

"Then what could have?"

Stephen looked around and then a glint of reflected light caught his eye. He looked down and spotted a piece of broken metal on the ground near the fallen warrior. He reached out and tried to pick it up only to receive a shock that felt like electricity.

"Did you find something?" Jack asked as he too reached down and touched the piece of metal only to get the same result. He gave Stephen a puzzled look.

"Hey Tori could you come here for a moment?" Stephen called out to his sister who was looking around nearby.

"Umm, sure." Victoria responded be joining the boys by the dead warrior.

"What do you make of that piece of metal?" Stephen asked as he pointed out the shard. Victoria shrugged and picked it up. She looked it over and handed it back to Stephen who discretely dropped it back on the ground as he couldn't hold it.

"Well that settles it. Judging by the little shock I got from touching it earlier and the damage dealt to its ribcage. That shard was from the broken gauntlets, Victoria used them at first and Groman after her."

"You mean..."

"Yeah. Groman was in this battle."

Chapter 11. Screams and Roars.

"What did you say?" Annie gasped as she hurried over to the two men.

"I said if my assessment is correct, Groman was a part of this battle. He took down this big guy at least. Probably more knowing his abilities." Stephen replied.

"So he is alive?" Annie murmured.

"I'd say the chances are pretty good so long as we don't find..." Jack began but Victoria cut him off before he could finish.

"Let's continue in the hope he still is alive and that we can catch up with him soon." Victoria added.

Annie and the others nodded in agreement then Saralia spoke up.

"Where do we go from here?"

"Keep going east I suppose," Dani answered. "Unless Monaria has any new advice for us."

Monaria looked down and shook her head slowly. "I have not had any new insight only that I feel that going east is still the right way to go."

"Good. I want to get as far away from here as possible." Dani shuddered.

"I agree young one. A battlefield is no place for a young lady," Urano said.

After quickly checking the rest of the battlefield for any survivors and finding none, the group continued their trek east as the sun began to set in front of them. As they made their way the trees began to increase in number and there were more and more rocky hills rolling over the landscape. The underbrush was surprisingly sparse with a few small berry bushes scattered about. The group kept mostly quiet except for Urano telling a few stories of his adventures to ease the tension they all felt after examining the battlefield.

As the sun began to fade away behind them, they found a small clearing and began to set up camp. Jack and Stephen dug a small hole and built a fire while the girls set about preparing food for their dinner. All the while Urano and Monaria were flying about making sure the area was clear.

After eating a little of the dried cliff crawler meat, the Ibexians had given them they began to doze off.

"I'll take first watch," Stephen said firmly.

"I'll take the next watch after a few hours," Jack added. "Just be sure to put the fire out. We don't want to attract any attention."

Stephen nodded and quickly buried the firepit with the loose dirt they had dug up. Soon everyone else was sleeping quietly in their bedrolls or against a tree. He couldn't help but chuckle when he noticed Monaria sleeping inside the hood of Dani's cloak.

"Must be pretty warm in that thing," He silently mused to himself. Just then he heard something large move to his right. He spun around, his hands grasping the Empty Sword, but he relaxed when he saw it was the half equine form of Saralia slowly walking towards him.

"Can't sleep?" He whispered.

"Not really," She replied quietly.

"Me either. That battlefield has had me on edge since we found it."

"I as well. Do you think they were attacking Groman?"

"I doubt it. The weapons we found were all a similar style. It was like two groups of the same tribe got into a fight and Groman was mixed up in it somehow. If they were all after Groman most of them would have similar injuries unless he picked up some of their weapons and used them too as well as the gauntlets."

"I have my doubts he would have been able to take them all down alone either."

"True. He may be good, but he's not that good. Unlike you."

"Please do not toy with me like that."

"I'm not. Saralia you might think that you're a failure after the test back there on the mountain. You're not, you got duped just like Jack and Tiny. Those snow-for-brains Ibexians set you up to fail. I'd be impressed if any of us could have won that fight. And you thew out two of them before they overwhelmed you! That is not a failure in my book."

Saralia swished her long tail while looking at the ground.

"Maybe, but I have been holding you all back this entire trip."

"Really? The way I see it you have not been holding us back. Despite being in places and situations that do not suit your skills or natural abilities you keep trying to help. Anyone else would have just called it quits and left but here you are, still trying to help. I think that is really impressive of you. You've really shown your true strength on this journey. Plus, you've been literally carrying all our extra stuff this entire time and you never seemed to even notice it or complain. I can't thank you enough for that."

Saralia trotted over to Stephen and hugged him.

"Thank you Stephen." She whispered before slowly going back to where she had been standing before. The two warriors stood there quietly looking at the shadows cast by the three moons. Stephen sighed and looked back at Saralia only to see she had turned white with fear.

"What's wrong Saralia?"

"You did not see that?"

"See what?"

"I just saw a shadow move from tree to tree!"

Stephen quickly scanned the treetops looking for anything out of the ordinary but saw nothing.

"Probably some small critter," He replied calmly.

Saralia sighed and swished her long tail. "I know what I saw!" She hissed. "There is something watching us!"

"You sure it wasn't something like a nutsnatcher? The forests back home are full of little critters that come out at night."

Saralia stomped a front hoof and crossed her arms. "I saw something much bigger than a small animal."

Stephen sighed again and looked around at the trees above him. He could just barely make out the shapes of the branches and limbs above him through the moonlight. Then he spotted something large sitting in the branches above where Annie was sleeping. He silently drew the Empty Sword and held it in both hands.

"Do you see it now?" Saralia smirked.

"You're right Saralia, I do see something. I'm not sure what though," Stephen replied. He then bent down and picked up a large nut that was lying at his feet. After tossing it up into the air and catching it again he threw it at the large shape in the tree branches. It smacked into the object causing it to fall for a few feet before being caught by some lower branches. Stephen sighed with relief and looked back at Saralia.

"Its just a dead branch. Probably blown loose in a storm."

Just as he was about to replace the Empty Sword into its sheath again, he heard something rustle directly above him. He looked up and saw a very dark shape in the branches about twenty feet above him. He thought it was another dead branch but then two glowing purple eyes opened within the figure and peered down at him.

"Who are you?" Stephen shouted. He was met by the most blood-curdling scream he had ever heard. The sleeping party was up in an instant as the silent forest gave way into a chorus of screaming as more and more pairs of glowing purple eyes appeared in the trees.

"It's an ambush! Run!" Jack shouted.

Saralia wasted no time in scooping up Dani and Annie and galloping away as fast as she could go dodging trees as she thundered along. Stephen, Jack, Tiny, and Victoria did their best to keep up with the Flitnao who were easily keeping up with the trodontian. Jack began to wheeze as he ran out of breath and Tiny slowed his pace, grabbed Jack and then threw him over his shoulder.

Stephen sensed something coming up behind and he drew the Empty sword and swung it around towards his attacker. He felt it connect with something that quickly fell to the ground. Not wanting to see what he had hit he kept running.

After a few more panic-stricken minutes of running, they came over a hill and spotted a rocky formation below them. Just as they reached it, they heard someone call out.

"In here!"

Tiny slid to a stop and the humans followed suit. When they looked behind them, they saw Saralia, Annie, and Dani waving at them from under a cluster of fallen trees that formed a sort of cave among the rocks. The group quickly ducked inside and crouched down. Tiny carefully moved a large tree trunk into the entrance and then backed away. The screams continued to get closer and soon filled their ears from all angles. Annie fell to her knees and started to shake uncontrollably.

"It is them! I know it is!" she cried in a panic.

Dani knelt down next to her and tried to calm her down. Just then they heard the sounds of talons clawing away at the tree trunks above them. Annie screamed and covered her face.

"They found us!" Jack shouted.

"I can see that!" Stephen replied.

"What do we do now?" Victoria shouted.

"We must fight our way out!" Urano shouted, drawing his sword.

"Can't you tell? There are way too many of them!" Jack shouted back.

"And it is only a matter of time before they dig their way in here somehow!" Saralia replied.

"I'm thinking!" Stephen called out. Just then a taloned hand burst through the cracks in the wood above them grasping for anything within reach. Annie and Dani screamed and backed away.

"No time! Tiny take monsters away!" Tiny said.

"And I will aid you!" Urano shouted.

Before anyone else could object Tiny kicked the tree trunk out of his way and charged out into the open air again. He looked up at the sky and let out the loudest roar he could manage before he and Urano raced away from the hiding place with a huge flock of the dark creatures in hot pursuit.

"Saralia, take Jack and Annie and run as fast as you can. We'll catch up!" Stephen shouted.

Jack opened his mouth to protest but with a quick look from Stephen he nodded in agreement and quickly got onto Saralia's back.

"But what about Tiny?" Dani objected.

"He'll be fine. Unkarians like him are really hard to kill!" Victoria replied as she took off at a sprint.

As they ran they could hear the creatures screaming and their calls being answered by loud incessant roars from Tiny. Stephen saw Saralia was beginning to slow down in front of them.

"Keep going! The farther we get from them the better! Tiny will catch up!"

Saralia nodded and was about to gallop away when they all heard Tiny roar once more. But this time just as he reached his loudest his roar was suddenly silenced like someone had turned his volume off. They all stared back where they had heard the sound come from. Victoria drew her claws and took a step towards the screams when Monaria flew up.

"Come on! They bought us some time! We cannot not waste it!"

The group broke into a run once more and kept up their pace for another fifteen minutes before they finally came to a stop at the edge of the forest near a cave mouth. Without saying a word, they hurried inside and huddled together. They waited there in the pitch darkness in silence listening to the screams fading away in the distance.

"They're gone," Jack panted.

"For now," Stephen said, gasping for air.

"But what about Tiny and Urano?" Annie asked quietly.

"I... I do not know," Saralia replied.

"We're going back for them, right?" Dani asked.

"Dani. I do not think it will be much use." Monaria said quietly.

"What do you mean? They are still out there!" Annie stood up quickly and walked over to the cave mouth before falling to her knees and cupping her face in her hands. Victoria and Monaria moved over to her and put their hands on her shoulders.

"He knew what he was doing. He died to keep us safe." Victoria said quietly.

"Urano did the same. He always has a plan to keep everyone else safe. After we found the bodies, he told me he felt that finding your brother is of the upmost importance," Monaria added.

"We can mourn for our friends tonight. But as Urano said earlier, I think Groman is the key to figuring out what is going on and stopping those creatures," Victoria said quietly.

"Their sacrifice will not be in vain," Jack said firmly.

The rest of the group nodded and began to settle down on the hard dirt floor. As Stephen lay on the ground, he could hear his sister and Annie softly crying themselves to sleep. He thought of the short time he knew Tiny and Urano. He knew they gave their lives to help them on their quest to save Groman and he had a feeling in his gut that once they did, they can make everything right again. He rolled over and felt the Empty Sword's scabbard jabbing his back. He sat up and unstrapped it from his back and looked the large blade over as he pulled it from the sheath. He read the inscription on the blade silently. 'A TRUE LEADER MUST HAVE A SERVANT'S HEART'.

"A true leader, and a true hero too." He thought quietly as he lay back down and fell asleep.

Chapter 12. An Abandoned Fortress.

The group awoke to sunlight pouring into their little hiding place and illuminating their tired faces. Victoria slowly stood up and looked at her friends and brother. Their faces showed signs of exhaustion from the night's run and their clothing was torn. In the panic they had left most of their supplies back at their camp. Thankfully they still had some of the dried meat in Saralia's saddlebags which she had not taken off the night before. But she knew it wouldn't last long. She checked her weapons was relieved that her tekko kagi claws were still in their sheaths at her sides.

"Does everybody else still have their weapons?" Jack asked.

"I think so," Dani answered as she checked her bow over.

"Is anybody else hurt?" Stephen asked as he tied a piece of cloth around a gash on his arm.

"I believe I am alright," Saralia said. She took a step forward and winced.

"You've got a decently-sized scratch on your left foreleg," Dani said as she quickly hurried over. She tore a small strip of cloth from the hem of her dress and tied it over the wound.

"Thank you, Dani," Saralia said quietly.

"We should get moving soon. I don't want to be in this forest when it gets dark again," Jack said firmly.

"I think we can all agree to that," Monaria said quietly.

After eating the remains of the dried meat, they had managed to bring with them, the seven remaining travelers cautiously ventured out into the open air again. Jack, Saralia, and Dani went out first, their bows and crossbow at the ready as they scanned the treetops for any more of the creatures.

"All clear!" Jack called back to the rest of the group, who slowly came out into the forest again.

"Alright, we need to keep going east," Stephen repeated.

"Are you sure we shouldn't go back?" Dani asked quietly.

"It would be of little use if we did. Those creatures most likely have taken our things back to their camp. And they would most undoubtedly be waiting for us if we went back to bury our fallen comrades," Monaria answered, wiping away a tear.

Dani and Annie nodded and then the group started off once more. Jack and Stephen took the lead with their weapons drawn, constantly looking around them for any more enemies. The girls stayed a short distance behind them with Annie riding on Saralia's back and Victoria and Monaria bringing up the rear. They continued their long journey though the seemingly endless forest for the entire morning and well into the afternoon. They only stopped a few times to rest and for Annie and Dani to switch places on Saralia's back. Almost the whole time they walked on nobody spoke, except to check to make sure everyone else was alright. So, it was when they came to an old dirt pathway did someone speak, almost scaring the others by breaking the silence.

"What's this? A pathway?" Jack asked in surprise.

"Looks like one to me," Stephen replied.

"Going by the large weeds growing around it, I would say it is not used very often except for the more recent boot prints going east," Saralia said.

"Boot prints? Not a taloned foot like the creatures we saw yesterday?" Victoria questioned.

"That's odd," Dani echoed.

"Well, since this path heads roughly east, should we follow it?" Jack asked.

"Yes." Monaria answered quickly. "We will find something important by the end of the day."

"Well, that's good enough for me, let's keep going." Stephen said as he started walking down the path, chopping weeds and bushes with his sword as he went.

The rest of the group quietly followed behind him and continued their slow march down the old dirt path. As they went, they noticed other, smaller, paths connecting to theirs, however they branched off in many different directions while theirs continued directly east. After a few more hours of walking, they came over a rise and saw something they were not expecting.

"A village!" Victoria exclaimed in surprise.

"It certainly looks like one," Jack added.

"Maybe we can find someone who can tell us what's going on!" Dani chimed in.

"I wouldn't be so hasty," Stephen said quickly.

"Why not?" Dani asked.

"We have little clue to who lives here. The creatures from last night may be the people who call this place home," Monaria answered.

Jack leaned forward and squinted at the distant houses. "I don't think anybody lives there. The houses are falling apart, and some are just piles of rubble in the street."

Stephen peered in the same direction and saw his friend was right. The village looked like nobody had lived in it for a long time, and now the forest was beginning to reclaim it.

"What's that just beyond the village?" Saralia asked.

Stephen looked harder and he could just barely make out a dark stone wall on the eastern edge of the village.

"It looks like a wall of some kind," He answered.

"It might be a fort or a castle," Jack added. "They would be often built near villages to better protect the people from attacks."

"Prarait had its own fort until they extended its walls to encompass the entire city," Saralia added.

"Well I'd say the fort might be as good a place as any to bed down for the night. The sun is beginning to set, and we don't know if those things will be looking for us." Stephen said.

"Well then we'd better get going if we are to make it there by dark," Victoria remarked.

"Right, but we had better be on the lookout just in case. Abandoned places rarely have anything good inside them," Jack said.

The group drew their weapons and carefully made their way into the deserted village. Soon they were surrounded by crumbling buildings and rotting market stalls. Stephen thought he could sense an air of something sinister hanging over them as they pushed on. That's when he felt Jack's hand on his shoulder. Jumping a bit in fright, he turned around and saw Jack was pointing at something.

"Do you see that stall?" Jack whispered.

"What about it?" Stephen hissed back.

"I don't think it fell due to age. It looks like someone or something big smashed it."

"Now that you mention it that house, we passed a few blocks ago did look like it was burned."

"Do you think this village was attacked?"

"Probably. Being so far out here in the middle of nowhere, any place could be an easy target for bandits or a marauding army."

"If the village is this bad, do you think the fort is still in one piece?"

"I don't know. But what other choice do we have? Camping outside is going to be near suicide with those things around. I wouldn't dare set foot in those deathtraps that used to be houses. If that fortress has a solid keep, we should be fine."

"If you say so."

"Will you two stop whispering? You're giving me the creeps," Victoria muttered as she pushed past them.

Slightly embarrassed, the two men hurried to keep up. Soon they came to a large set of heavy wooden gates set into the twenty-foot-high stone wall. Saralia tried pulling them open but to no avail.

"They must be barred from the other side," Annie remarked.

"Well how are we going to get through then?" Dani asked.

Before anyone could answer Monaria quickly flew to the top of the wall, took a look over before racing back to the group and motioning for them to follow her. They quickly obeyed and ducked out of sight of the stone walls.

"There is a small group of guards along the walls!" She whispered.

"What?" Victoria gasped in surprise.

"It was not what I was expecting either," Monaria replied.

"Well, that complicates things. What else did you see?" Stephen said.

Monaria flew over to a windowsill and sat down. "There are about a dozen of those same creatures patrolling the walls and a few more guarding the entrance of the keep.

"How big was the keep?" Jack asked.

"Only about two stories tall," Monaria answered.

"That doesn't seem very big," Stephen replied.

"Doesn't matter right now. What matters is should we even try to get in?" Jack asked.

"We must," Monaria replied.

"What?" Victoria responded.

"Someone important is in there." Monaria said before going limp on the windowsill. Annie scooped her up gently and laid her inside one of the pouches on her belt.

"Well how do we get in?" Annie said with a determined tone.

"We can check to see if there are any ladders lying around. Or find a way to break the gates in," Saralia suggested.

"We don't want to alert the guards. Especially if there are more hiding within the keep," Stephen added.

"If I can get to the top of the wall, I may be able to find a sally port and let you in," Victoria said.

"Sally port?" Dani asked.

"A small gate designed for livestock, and spies," Jack answered quickly.

"Thanks," Dani whispered.

"Back to what I was saying, if I can get up there, I'm pretty sure I can let you in somehow," Victoria finished.

"Before we do. I think we should send little flyer to get help." Annie said. "He has been sleeping in my pocket for a while now and should be ready to fly again." She pulled the red lizard out of its hiding place and looked it in the eyes. "Go get help." She whispered before tossing it into the air. The little lizard chirped before zooming away.

"Good idea. At least if we were to be captured help would be coming eventually" Jack said.

Saralia poked her head out and looked at the wall. "Looks like it is about twenty feet high. Victoria how much do you weigh?"

"Why do you want to know?" Victoria asked defensively.

Without answering Saralia quickly grabbed her by the collar and belt and threw her up towards the top of the wall. Just before she fell back down, she managed to grab the top of the wall.

"Give me a warning next time!" She hissed before pulling herself up and over the top. The group heard the sounds blades being drawn and someone grunt in pain before the body of a guard was pushed over the wall where it fell.

"I see a door about twenty feet to the south. You'd better be there when I open it," Victoria whispered.

"You heard her," Stephen said with a shrug.

The group quickly rushed along the wall and soon found the door just where Victoria had told them. They could hear two guards walking around on the other side of the door. Just then they heard Victoria's claws hit the guards as she hit the ground. Then they heard another guard call out moments before he met his end by Victoria's blades. After another minute the gate was pushed open and Victoria beckoned her comrades inside. Stephen looked over his sister's handiwork with a grimace.

"Those guards didn't stand a chance," He muttered.

"I gave them more of a chance than they gave Tiny," She hissed back before running up the stone steps to the top of the wall. Soon more guards where rushing towards them. Their glowing purple eyes standing out against their dark armor and plumage.

"Stop them!" another guard called out as he flew towards them.

Saralia had her bow drawn in a second and soon the attacker was falling with an arrow in its head.

"That was for our friends," She growled as she laid another arrow on the string. Victoria was busy running along the walls as she took down any guards who were too slow to take off while the others were dealing with any remaining guards. Suddenly the air became full of screaming as guards poured out of the upper story of the keep.

"There's too many of them!" Jack called out as he dropped another birdman.

"We won't make it there in time!" Stephen called back as he threw his dagger at a guard, killing it instantly. He drew The Empty Sword from its sheath and held it aloft over his head. Suddenly all the guards stopped in their tracks and stared at Stephen.

"What are they doing?" Dani asked in bewilderment.

Victoria sprinted over and rejoined the group, her look of confusion mirroring their own. Stephen waved the Empty Sword around defiantly as the guards held their position.

"What do we do now?" Jack asked.

He was answered by the sound of deafening laughter coming from all around them.

"What to do indeed?" The voice boomed. "How about you listen to me and bring me that shiny sword? If you do, you may just keep your lives. Do not worry; I am not far away, I am in the keep. My men will leave you alone unless you misbehave."

"And what if we don't want to?" Stephen shouted.

At once all the guards drew their weapons and within seconds nearly a hundred arrows were aimed at the party.

"You had to ask," Victoria growled.

"Alright alright, we will come to you." Saralia shouted.

"Very wise. I will even open the door for you," The voice said with a laugh.

The group looked over at the keep and saw its large wooden doors slowly swing open. The guards parted for them to enter the keep.

"Come in my little warriors! Do not keep me waiting..."

"We're all agreed that this is a trap, right?" Jack asked in a whisper.

"It is most certainly a trap. But what other choice do you have?" The voice answered with a laugh. "Now come in, before I change my mind and stop being so friendly."

Chapter 13. Confrontation.

The group slowly made their way towards the ominous gateway into the keep with trepidation. As they made their way through the lines of guards Victoria couldn't help but steal a glance at the soldiers who had been fighting them only moments before. The guards were staring straight ahead, their glowing purple eyes not seeming to give the adventurers a second look. She thought about their chances of survival if they were to begin the attack again once they were inside the keep. While they would have the stone walls and heavy wooden gates between them and the outside she didn't know if there were even more guards just inside the keep. The disembodied voice also gave her worry. She didn't know who or what it was much less how powerful it was.

"What's our plan?" Jack whispered.

"We just need to do what the voice was saying. If we try to fight back, we'll be overwhelmed in seconds." Stephen whispered back.

"Yes. Listen to the voice of reason." The voice laughed.

"Looks like he can hear us no matter how quiet we are." Dani said.

"You are correct little one. There is no hiding from me. Now please come inside, I grow tired of waiting."

The group stood for a moment before finally walking inside the great stone keep. As soon as they entered the gates swung closed behind them, nearly catching Saralia's tail and making her jump forwards. Once she had calmed down, they all looked around at the room they were in. It was a large stone room with a stone staircase leading up to the second story illuminated by sporadic torches hanging from the walls on hooks. But what got everyone's attention immediately wasn't the two dozen guards who stood around them and the further dozen at the top of the stairs it was the wide staircase that led down into the ground just in front of them.

"Come down to me." The voice echoed.

"Do what it says. Just keep the weapons at the ready." Stephen whispered.

The others nodded and began to slowly make their way down the stairs into the depths of the keep. After descending the stairs into the lower level into what looked like a dungeon, they found there was another staircase that continued deeper.

"Keep going my little friends." The voice giggled. "Just a little further and we shall meet face to face."

The group kept going down into the dimly lit passageway. At the bottom of the stairs, they found a narrow hallway that led to a small doorway.

"Come in! Come in!" The voice echoed from the other side of the door.

The group made their way towards the small wooden door and slowly opened it to reveal a dark room on the other side.

"Umm I am sorry, but I do not think I can fit through that doorway. It is too short." Saralia said hesitantly.

"Can't you duck under it?" Stephen asked.

Saralia shook her head. "I am not that flexible."

Just then the group saw more of the guards slowly moving down the stairs towards them, their weapons drawn.

"If you continue to make me wait, I will have my men give you some encouragement. Do not worry about your trodontian friend. She will be safe if she behaves." The voice called from the other room.

"You heard it. Just leave me here, I will be fine. Besides," Saralia patted the hilts of her scimitars. "If they try anything, I have been itching for a rematch."

"If you say so," Dani replied.

"Please be careful Sara," Victoria said.

"I will. Go and show this person you mean business. I shall hold the line on this end." Saralia replied before turning to face the guards who were now moving down the hallway.

The rest of the group ducked under the doorway and into the darkened room. As soon as they were inside, they hear the door slam shut behind them making them jump.

"Welcome to my lair." The voice laughed.

"Who are you?" Stephen shouted. He drew the Empty Sword from its sheath on his back and tried to keep his hands from shaking.

"Where are you?" Victoria echoed, clenching her tekko kagi claws so tightly her knuckles turned white.

"Allow me to answer both questions at once." The voice called out. Suddenly a loud hissing was heard at the back of the room. The group turned to see a glowing, red-hot sword being plunged into a trough. Quickly flames burst from the trough and ran around the edges of the room illuminating it with a fiery glow. It was a large room with no furniture or anything ornate within it. The floors, walls and ceiling were made of plain stone blocks and there was a heavy wooden door at the other end. But what held their attention the most was a black cloaked figure that stood just in front of the other door. Its heavy hooded cloak covered most of the figure's features aside from it being nearly six feet tall and its weapon. Its sword was a two-handed great sword which had a black blade with glowing red cracks running down it.

"Boss fight?" Jack whispered to Stephen.

"Boss fight," Stephen replied lowering the Empty Sword in a ready position.

The figure laughed heartily and stared at the group. "I see my scouts were right all along. It is you."

"You know us?" Victoria said quizzically.

"Oh yes, I know you. And I am hurt by the fact you do not remember me." The figure said in a mocking tone before looking at Annie. "Especially you, little traitor."

Annie's face went white with shock. "Elder Narrot?" She gasped.

The figure laughed as he pulled down his hood to reveal a young kittrian man with a twisted scar over his left eye and an evil grin. Though the group noticed his eyes were a bright purple instead of their former orange. "So, you do remember me after all."

"Who is he?" Dani whispered.

"He is the one who turned me in for helping Steve and Tori escape his trap." Annie replied.

"You're the elder who tried to trick us into getting captured on our second night!" Stephen shouted back.

"You're the reason Annie was captured and nearly killed!" Victoria screamed.

"That is correct, though she is the reason I nearly lost my left eye. My old master was rather upset about my inability to capture you. When I learned of your little meeting in the woods from one of my agents, I knew I had to get rid of you. I am disappointed you survived your imprisonment." Narrot scowled. "After my old master was defeated, I fled to the north where I found this sword. A voice told me I should take it as it was meant for me, and it also told me that I needed to lure those monsters towards the little city. After that was done, I came here, and I have been waiting for you since."

"What do you want from us?" Dani asked.

"Straight to the point, I like her." Narrot chuckled. "I want the Empty Sword."

"Come and take it. Only the chosen ones can wield it." Stephen growled.

"You overestimate your abilities; you think you are an invincible warrior incapable of losing. Yet you have lost so much in your time here.

You lost several battles, you broke your weapons many times, and you have lost so many friends and allies."

"Shut up!" Stephen shouted.

"So many trodontian warriors at Altimi and the battles afterwards. Your unkarian and feeble friend the other night. Falamore had to give his life to save yours. And lest we forget, your sister's near-death at the hands of my old master. You could not save her then, let see if you can save..." He was cut off by Stephen screaming in rage and rushing towards him. Narrot merely stepped aside and watched Stephen nearly run into the heavy wooden door. In a moment Narrot swung his own sword at Stephen's head, Stephen ducked and watched the blade embed itself into the wood. Stephen kicked Narrot in the chest sending him backwards without his sword. Stephen heard a hissing above him and saw to his surprise the wood around the sword was beginning to smolder and burn. He turned his attention back to Narrot who was now on the ground surrounded by his friends, their weapons drawn.

"Surrender, you're outnumbered and outgunned." Jack shouted.

"No! You cannot defeat me like this! I was told I would crush all before me!" Narrot cried. He hit the ground with his left foot and the group heard a sharp metallic click.

"Boot knife!" Jack called out as he jumped back and fired his crossbow missing Narrot by inches. Narrot swung his foot out towards Dani's legs, but Annie stepped in the way. The knife clashed into her prosthetic leg bending the blade and rendering it useless. Narrot stared at his broken weapon in disbelief before looking into Annie's stern face.

"That trick does not work on me anymore." Annie said coldly. "Thanks to you."

"Nice move Annie!" Dani cheered.

Stephen lowered the Empty Sword and held the tip at Narrot's neck. "Surrender," He growled. "Nothing would give us greater pleasure than to beat you within an inch of your sorry life and leave you for the monsters outside. Now give up! I won't ask again."

"I... I... Master!" Narrot cried out, his voice echoing in the stone chamber.

Suddenly the group heard the wooden door behind them open slowly and another figure in a dark green cloak emerged.

"It is not he who should be surrendering young warriors, it is you." The figure's voice boomed as it stared at them with glowing purple eyes.

"And there's the true final boss." Stephen said firmly.

The adventurers stood facing the hooded figure. their weapons at the ready. Monaria hovered just behind them keeping her rapier point firmly at Narrot's neck. The figure laughed as it looked them over.

"I've been waiting for this ever since I heard about the defeat of the Shadowed One." His eyes closed as he inhaled deeply. "I can sense the power within that sword, so much power, some of which hasn't even been exploited yet. And to have it brought to my doorstep? This is a good day!"

"What are you talking about?" Stephen shouted. He gripped the Empty Sword even tighter and held firm as Victoria stepped by his side.

"However, I sense that the true wielder of this blade is not here. You are only able to wield it due to some freak accident." The figure turned to Narrot who was still on the ground in fear. "Why didn't you bring him Narrot?"

"My master, I have been trying to lure him here. But he has found allies in the remaining Horition clans. Our men have yet to defeat them in battle. I need more time." Narrot pleaded.

The figure looked over at the still glowing sword that was stuck in the door and slowly reached out and grasped the hilt. His hand shook as he pulled it out and admired the glowing red pattern on the blade. But as he held it the sword began to lose its glow and the black blade began to turn a dull grey. Soon it had become just like any normal sword. The figure dropped it and it shattered into a dozen pieces when it hit the stone floor.

"Time? We have little time. The man I sent you to find will be here soon and I am not ready to defeat him yet! I need more power before I can truly best him! You have failed me for the last time!" The figure boomed.

Narrot quickly got to his knees and started sobbing. "Please master! Spare me! I will do anything you ask!"

The figure looked at Narrot and his glowing eyes narrowed and switched from violet to red within the hood. "Despite your other failures, you did bring me another of the ancient tools. For that I will give you the reward... Of a quick death."

Instantly a wall of fire erupted from the figure's hands and towards the group who all dodged the attack except for Narrot. Narrot screamed for help seconds before he was incinerated instantly by the flames. Dani and Annie screamed and leapt away from where Narrot had knelt only moments before.

"What did you do?" Victoria screamed.

"You asked what I was talking about earlier, well I am on a quest of sorts. I am collecting as many of the ancient weapons and tools this world has to offer and draining them of their power. Soon I will be unstoppable to even the most powerful warriors, even the chosen one." The figure said in a calm tone.

"But why?" Stephen asked.

"Simple. When I came to this world decades ago, I learned many things. I learned about the ancient tools and weapons that were supposedly left by the 'god' of this world for the protection and service of the tribes. I learned that the entire land doesn't have any one ruler, instead it is made up of various tribes of backwards creatures who are constantly squabbling with each other. Then I learned how I could harness the power of the artifacts and use them as my own. That is when I, Falron the Feared, decided to begin my quest of finding the artifacts and using their power to unite this world under my sovereign rule!" Falron answered.

"Falron the feared?" Monaria asked, puzzled.

"I have never heard of you before." Annie added.

Falron laughed again before removing his hood and revealing his face. He was a human like Stephen, Jack, Victoria, and Dani. He had square chin and jawline, small nose, short white hair, and his eyes switched from red to violet again.

"You're from..." Stephen started.

"Earth." Falron finished. "Yes, I stumbled into this world by accident while on the run from some, shall we say, marshals? I had finally escaped from the hole they put me in because of my beliefs on how to make the world a better place."

"You're an escaped convict?" Jack asked in surprise. Falron laughed in response.

"Enough about me. I want to offer you a deal. You give me that sword right now. And I'll let you rule alongside me as my officers and generals. I'll even show special favors to the Flitnao and Kittrian people." He added while looking at Annie and Monaria.

"What if we refuse to take the deal?" Stephen said gritting his teeth. He knew this would be bad, but they had no other right option.

"Then you will be forced into giving it to me by less-than-gentle methods." Falron replied with a chuckle.

"Come and take it then!" Stephen shouted while raising the Empty Sword above his head.

"Oh, I won't take it from you. You will give it to me." Falron laughed mocking as he raised his hands and held them out towards the group. His eyes switched from violet to a deep purple as a blast of purple energy shot from his fingertips and rushed towards Stephen. Stephen swung The Empty Sword downwards and tried to deflect the blast with its blade. To his horror he saw the blade merely divided the blast which went around him and hit Victoria, Jack, and Monaria. The three of them cried out in pain before falling to the ground with Annie managing to catch Monaria before she hit the floor. Dani rushed to check on Victoria and Jack, she quickly checked their pulses before looking up at Stephen, her eyes filling with tears. Stephen stared at his fallen sister and friends in shock before Falron's laugh got his attention.

"Oh dear, you've gone and made a mess of things, didn't you?" Falron snickered.

"I'm going to kill you for that!" Stephen shouted as he ran towards Falron noticing his eyes switching to red. Falron shot a fire blast at Stephen which he managed to block with his shield. Once Falron's attack let up Stephen looked up to see Falron had slipped away back behind the wooden door he had come from.

"Come back here you coward!" Stephen roared, pounding on the heavy door with all his strength.

"I wouldn't bother with me right now. You're about to be too busy to care." Falron's voice echoed from behind the door.

Stephen then heard a moaning from behind him and he spun around to see Dani jumping away from their fallen comrades who were now slowly rising to their feet. He dropped his shield and quickly sheathed his sword before rushing over to help Victoria to her feet while Dani helped Jack.

"Tori! Thank God! I thought you were gone!" Stephen cried as he gave his sister a tight hug. The he heard something that made his blood run cold. He heard the sounds of blades being drawn and he quickly pushed Victoria away. To his horror he saw she had her tekko kagi claws out and ready for action, while her face was still looking towards the ground.

"Jack! What are you doing? It's me! Dani! Dani Wyng!" Dani screamed, and Jack drew his own sword and slowly began walking towards her, his own face still staring at the ground.

Stephen quickly glanced over and saw Monaria had also drawn her own weapon and was beginning to force Annie into a corner. Then all three of them began to laugh in unison and they looked up at their friends to reveal their eyes had begun to glow a bright purple.

"This cannot be happening! Annie cried, as she ducked under the sweep of Monaria's blade.

The three possessed heroes laughed and spoke as one. "I assure you my dears that it can. The first artifact I found was the crown of some long-forgotten Flitnao king who had the power to make everyone obey him. While the crown wouldn't fit my on my head, it did make a good ring. And with its power I have amassed an army from the nearby tribes, worthy of storming the strongest citadel! Now you get to die at the hands of your own friends!"

"Let them go!" Stephen roared as he raced for the door again. Before he even reached it, he saw Victoria gracefully flip over him and land in a crouching position, ready to strike. "Fight him, Tori! I don't want to hurt you!"

"But I want to hurt you!" Victoria replied as she lashed out with her claws narrowly missing Stephen's chest. She swung again only for Stephen to block her attack with The Empty Sword. As their blades remained locked Stephen heard Dani scream from behind him. He risked a quick glance over his shoulder and saw her ducking out of the way of Jack's blade nearly taking some hair off the top of her head. He tried to look for Annie but couldn't see her anywhere, but Monaria was busy flying around trying to find her. Stephen then felt the pressure on his sword release, and he quickly turned around to see Victoria resuming her attack swinging her claws wildly. "You're always trying to hold me back! You always think I need protection when we fight! Now who's the one who needs protecting?" Victoria screamed as she continued her attack.

Stephen did his best to block the wild strikes, but he knew it was only a matter of time before Victoria got a hit in. He thought if he could drop the Empty sword and grab his shield, he might buy himself a few more seconds. He held the heavy Empty sword with his right hand and drew his one-handed sword with his left blocking Victoria's attempts to stab him. Their blades locked once again Stephen risked another glance to see where his shield was. To his surprise he didn't see it anywhere.

"Dani where's my shield?" He shouted.

"I'm kinda busy right now!" Dani replied as she dodged another attack from Jack.

Just then the two of them heard a loud bang and they saw Monaria fall to the ground unconscious, the purple light gone out of her eyes.

"Dani! Keep Jack busy for a few more minutes! With his asthma he'll tire out soon!" Stephen shouted as he kicked Victoria back a few paces.

"That's what I am trying to do!"

Dani backed up another step and tripped over a loose stone and fell on her backside. Jack was standing over her in an instant and he quickly thrust his sword down trying to pin her to the ground.

"You have no hope!" Jack said. "You've always been the weaker one of us."

Dani scooted backwards quickly, and the sword tip just caught the edge of her dress. Dani tore herself away and stood up only to hear Jack taunting her again.

"Just give up and let Falron take over for you. He can take away all your pain and weaknesses."

"Not all of them. Dani replied grimly. She could already hear Jack beginning to struggle for air. Thinking fast, she ducked low and swept his legs out from under him and he fell to the ground.

"Physical strength isn't everything. I've been through a lot more than you even know. But the fact I am still going and trying to be a better person shows where my true strength really is!"

Jack jumped to his feet but swayed unsteadily before some invisible object smashed into him, knocking him back to the floor. Dani watched as the purple light in his eyes went out and Jack groaned in pain. She looked around for what had knocked Jack out.

"Annie?" Dani asked.

"I am here." Annie's voice came from thin air. "I have Steve's shield, it is kittrian made so I can make it vanish too. I knocked Monaria out with it. Now I need you to help Steve with Tori so I can knock her out too."

Dani nodded, grabbed Jack's sword, and rushed to Steve's aid only to have him block her with his blade.

"Stay back, both of you, this is my fight." Stephen said calmly. He dropped both the Empty Sword and his own one-handed sword and faced his sister. "I know what I need to do."

Victoria laughed and charged at Stephen, her claws lowered, ready to run him through. Stephen stood his ground and waited until her claws were nearly at his chest. Then he deftly turned his body and grabbed her arms. Using her momentum, he swung her around and into a wall. She slammed into it and fell to the ground, and he quickly pinned her down.

"Listen Tori. I know you're still in there. You need to fight him! You're much more stubborn than that!" Stephen grunted as Victoria kept trying to squirm free of his grasp.

"If you think I am so strong than why do you hold me back?" She screamed.

"Because I don't want to see you get hurt again!" Stephen's voice echoed in the stone chamber. "I couldn't handle seeing you get hurt by the Shadowed One, so I have been trying to keep you safe. If you were to get hurt again, I don't know what I would do. That's why you need to break free of Falron's control. I know you can!"

Victoria let out a bloodcurdling scream and threw Stephen off before quickly trying to stand up only to be hit in the face with the invisible shield. She dropped to the ground and Stephen breathed a sigh of relief as the purple glow faded from her eyes.

"I am so sorry Tori." Annie said as she appeared kneeling next to her.

"Yes, you are going to be sorry child." Falron's voice boomed as he entered the room with over a dozen guards. "Since my new minions failed it looks like I will have to deal with you all myself!"

Chapter 14. Hello and Goodbye.

Falron surveyed the room with his arms folded. "I'm impressed that you were able to break my control so easily. However, you will find that these men are not so easily turned." Falron laughed as the guards attacked.

Stephen lunged for The Empty Sword and managed to grasp its hilt moments before the first guard was upon him. He quickly dodged the attack and stabbed the guard through the chest only to watch in disbelief as it dissolved into dust around the blade and disappeared. Before he was able to process what he had just seen, he heard Dani scream for help. He turned to see she was running away from three of the guards while trying to get an arrow on the string of her bow. Monaria, Victoria, and Jack were still unconscious on the ground and Annie was trying to keep the guards back by swinging her dagger around wildly. He then felt a taloned hand grasp his shoulder and without looking he swung the Empty Sword backwards and into the guard who also dissolved into dust.

"There's too many of them!" Stephen shouted.

Falron began to laugh once more as the three remaining heroes fought for their lives. "I don't just have to possess people to grow my army, I can make dark doppelgangers of them too!"

Falron's laugh was interrupted by a loud bang on the wooden door the heroes had come through. Everyone, even Falron and his clones stopped and looked at the door. Then a rear hoof burst through the door making a small hole in the wood and a tiny figure flew through.

"Stop right there in the name of Urano, commander of the Flitnao fighters!" Urano shouted, pointing his sword at Falron.

Falron responded by laughing again. "You have an even worse chance of defeating me, puny warrior, what makes you think you have any hope of beating my army?"

"I know I can defeat you, whoever you are, Because of one reason." Urano replied. Suddenly the wall around the door gave way, causing a cloud of dust and dirt to rise from the rubble. Saralia jumped through the dust and landed near her fallen comrades, she quickly laid an arrow on her bowstring and aimed at Falron.

"Army? More like more target practice! What do you think Tiny?" Saralia called out as the massive form of Tiny crouched through the hole and then stood up in the room.

"Tiny crush shadow things!" Tiny roared.

Falron's face looked momentarily worried before he raised his arms and laughed as nearly two dozen more shadow guards appeared around him. "Your friends cannot defeat me! My army is infinite!"

"Wanna bet?" Stephen growled as he watched Victoria and Jack slowly get to their feet, their eyes back to normal.

"I call dibs on the mad wizard." Jack grumbled as he loaded his crossbow.

"You'll have to beat me to him." Victoria replied as she readied her claws.

"I'll go high you two go low." Monaria shouted as she rose in the air.

Falron's face went pale as he summoned even more of the shadow guards. "Come and take me then!" He shouted.

"Enough!" A familiar voice boomed from the hallway.

Stephen felt a tug on the Empty Sword and suddenly it wrenched itself from his hands and flew backwards towards the opening in the wall. Then a green-skinned, six-fingered hand reached up and caught it by the hilt before its true master entered the room with an army of the strange bird-like people behind him.

The figure was nearly as tall as Jack but more muscularly built and stocky. He was dressed in leather armor worn over a red tunic, brown trousers, and boots. He had a firm but friendly face and piercing blue eyes with narrow cat-like pupils. A familiar crimson winged lizard was perched on his shoulder. Upon seeing Annie it flew to her and up her sleeve again.

"Groman!" Annie cried out before rushing her brother and nearly tackling him with a hug.

"Annie? What in the name of The One Above are you doing here?" Groman responded in surprise. He looked up and saw the four humans who were now looking back at him. "Steve? Tori? And who are these two?"

"Fight now talk later!" Jack shouted as he steadied his crossbow aiming for Falron's head.

Falron laughed and shook his head. "It seems you all have some catching up to do. As I am not ready to fight you yet I will leave you for now. However, Groman, is it? We will meet again. Do not think you or your family will be safe from me. I have eyes and ears everywhere and I can assure you, I will return. And when I do, I will be more powerful than any of you can imagine!" Falron then waved his right hand and the shadow guards turned to dust which began to blow around the room blocking him from view.

"He's getting away!" Victoria shouted.

Jack, Dani, and Saralia loosed their arrows at where Falron was standing only to hear them hit the opposite wall. Soon the dust settled down and they all couldn't see any trace of Falron or even the door he had escaped through.

Stephen stomped his foot in annoyance. "Great! he disappeared."

"Have your men search the forests and village outside. I will join you shortly." Groman said to a nearby birdman who quickly ran back out through the hole Tiny had made.

Stephen breathed a sigh of relief that the threat was over before feeling himself and nearly everyone else being crushed in a bear hug.

"Tiny's friends! Tiny so happy to see you!" Tiny said happily.

"It's good to see you too Tiny!" Dani giggled.

"Could you let us go? I can barely breathe." Jack wheezed.

Tiny released his crushing grip and the humans and Annie dropped to the floor.

"What happened Tiny? We thought you were..." Victoria started but was interrupted by Urano.

"Dead? No my friends. Tiny merely had his throat slashed by one of those shadow beasts and could not speak for some time. I fought to keep him safe while he healed from his wounds and then we followed your tracks here." Urano replied.

"Speaking of that. Who are they?" Stephen asked.

"We are the Horiton. We have lived peacefully in the forests east of the swamps for generations before Falron arrived and either enslaved our people under his control or made copies of us to serve as his army." One of the Horiton answered. "We learned of the chosen one being found in the lands to the south thanks to a Flitnao seer and we set out to recruit his aid in dealing with this menace. While we were successful, Falron had also sent some of his own forces to attack the city where he was staying, and we had to resort to... less ideal methods."

"You mean you kidnapped my brother just so he can fight for you?" Annie nearly shouted.

"Yes. We deeply regret what we did that night. We hope you can forgive us as your brother has."

Annie looked over at her brother in a mixture of surprise and disbelief.

"They needed help Annie. If I had known, I would have come up here on my own anyways. That is what I am supposed to do as the chosen one." Groman said softly.

Annie looked down at the ground. "So that thing that attacked me, wasn't one of you?"

"No, it was merely one of our brethren controlled by that monster Falron."

"Then, I forgive you too."

The Horiton warrior nodded solemnly before exiting the room and everyone else began to follow him back up the stairs and into the fading sunlight. After a few moments of silence Stephen spoke up.

"Groman, these are our friends from our world, Jack and Dani. And these are two Flitnao fighters who aided us on our quest to find you, Urano and Monaria.

"It is good to meet you all. And it is very good to see you again Steve and Tori." Groman replied.

"I... It's great to see you again too." Victoria said with a bit of a stammer. Stephen raised a quizzical eyebrow but shrugged and said nothing when he saw his sister's reddening face.

"So, what do we do now?" Jack asked.

"I can ask the Horiton to fly you back to Lulandal." Groman said. "It will only take them a few hours to fly you to your gateway home. Though I am afraid they cannot help Tiny and Saralia."

"That is fine. I do not mind walking." Saralia said quietly.

"Tiny like walking through forest. Make Tiny think of home." Tiny added.

"What about you Groman? Aren't you coming back with us?" Victoria asked. "We did come all this way just to find you after all."

Groman stopped walking and looked away towards the setting sun. "I cannot. I am needed here. Falron will be back, and it is my duty to protect the lands from whatever threat may befall them."

"But... but..." Annie whimpered before running over to her brother again and clasping his arm in her hands. "I do not want to lose you again."

Groman pulled her in for a hug. "Nor I you, but right now I do not think it would be wise for you to stay with me. You heard Falron yourself. Nobody is safe." Groman looked up at Stephen and Victoria. "Except for you."

"What do you mean?" Stephen asked.

"Can we talk privately?" Groman asked.

Victoria nodded and she, Stephen and Groman walked a short distance from the group.

"I am sure you two have done a lot for me in the past few weeks, and while I would hate to ask more of you..." Groman began but was cut off by Stephen.

"You want us to take Annie back to our world, don't you?"

Victoria let out a little gasp as Groman slowly nodded. "I know she will be safest there. Falron will come back and if The One Above wills it, I will defeat him. But in the time that it will take to track him down I do not want him to try and kidnap or harm Annie. That is why I am asking you to promise to make sure she will be well taken care of in your world. I know it will be very hard for her to be away from Lulandal, but I pray it will not be for a very long time."

"I..." Victoria started before being cut off by Groman.

"Please promise me that you will keep her safe." He then looked at Stephen. "Remember what you told me on your last visit. Please do the same for me as I would do for you."

Stephen slowly nodded. "I promise that I will do everything within my power to make sure Annie stays safe."

Groman sighed. "Thank you."

The trio began to walk back to the rest of the group who were talking to some of the Horiton warriors.

"Let us know when we can return with Annie." Stephen said quietly.

"The sooner we can come back the better." Victoria added to which Stephen raised an eyebrow. "I don't know how well Annie will fit in our world. There are a lot of things to get used to over there." She quickly added as Stephen rolled his eyes.

When they rejoined the group Groman went over to a Horiton who appeared to be the leader of the army while Stephen and Victoria said their goodbyes to Saralia and Tiny.

"Tiny hope to see you again soon." Tiny said as a tear ran down his stony grey cheek.

"I'll miss you too Tiny." Victoria replied.

"Thank you, Tiny. For everything. You've been a big help for me." Dani added.

Tiny leaned down and scooped the little girl up in another hug before setting her back down.

"Sara, I hope you have a safe trip back to Lulandal." Stephen said.

"As do I. I have had enough adventures to last me a while." Saralia replied.

"Be sure to let the Ibexians know that we were unable to recover their sword before it was destroyed. And let the other tribes and cities know to prepare for war with Falron still on the loose." Jack added.

"Tiny will tell them." Tiny said confidently.

"We will make sure we are ready for whatever may come." Saralia added.

"Good," Stephen said.

"Well my fine warrior friends I wish you a safe and fortunate journey back to your homelands." Urano said.

"It was an honor to fight alongside you." Jack replied giving the tiny warrior a salute which Urano returned.

"We will meet again." Monaria said with a smile.

"You're sure of that?" Victoria asked.

"Quite sure."

"I will look forward to it then."

Then the two flitnao took off into the sunset and Tiny and Saralia waved and began to walk out of the old fortress courtyard.

Annie remained silent throughout the goodbyes and keep staring at Groman as he returned to the remaining adventurers.

"The Horiton have agreed to fly you all home. Are you ready to go?" Groman said quietly.

Annie burst into tears and ran towards Groman and hugged him tightly. "Please do not send me away! I do not want to be apart from you again!" She buried her face in his tunic and sobbed.

Groman's eyes began to water as he looked down at his sister. "I did not want to do this either. But it is the only way for you to be safe. Steve and Tori will make sure to take care of you while I am away."

"You are sending me... with them? Into their world?" Annie whimpered.

"Falron will be searching for any way he can get to me. With his powers he can go almost anywhere or control anyone. No place here or in Lulandal is safe anymore. Sending you to a place outside his control with people I trust is the best option I have."

"But... but..."

"I will miss you too Annalio, so very much. Seeing you again has renewed my strength and resolve to finish this battle as soon as I can. And once I do, I will send for you to return."

Annie sniffed and reached into the sleeve of her dress, pulling out the drowsy, red, flying lizard who chirped in protest. "Then... you will need little flyer more than I will."

Groman let out a little chuckle as the lizard chirped again and jumped onto his shoulders. "I will send him as soon as I know it is safe for you to return."

"Please be careful Groman."

"I will Annalio."

With that the two siblings embraced and shed a few tears before separating. Annie climbed onto the back of a waiting Horiton and watched as the humans shook hands with Groman before climbing on their own horiton. As they took off Stephen and Victoria waved back at Groman, Annie kept her eyes forward.

Their flight through the ever-darkening skies was uneventful. Nobody talked much other than to give their friendly rides directions on where to go. Soon they had crossed the mountains and were flying over the lands of Lulandal. Stephen tried to point out places where they had been on his and Victoria's previous journey. While Dani and Jack simply enjoyed the view of the land below them lit by the triple moons.

Soon they began to descend towards the forest and Stephen pointed out a clearing for them to land in. Once they were on the ground, they thanked the Horiton who took off once more into the night sky.

"What now?" Jack asked quietly.

"We head back to the wooded pathway and go home." Stephen said. "I can see it right over there."

"What about our stuff and your great-aunt's sword?" Dani asked.

"I told the elder to have someone leave your things by the entrance to your world." Annie answered quietly.

"Well then let's go home." Jack said.

The group began to walk towards the pathway, but Annie stayed back taking one last look at the familiar forest. Victoria turned around to look as well, when she saw Annie still standing there, she walked back to her.

"I do not want to leave." Annie said quietly. "What if Groman needs me?"

"I know he would tell us if he did. And I can tell you this, if he does need our help, you can be sure that Steve and I will do everything within our power to get back here and help." Victoria answered. "I promise."

Annie looked up at Victoria and managed a weak smile. "I know you will."

"Hey! I found our stuff!" Jack called out from the wooden tunnel.

"Looks like we are near my home, are you ready?" Victoria asked.

"No, but we should go anyway." Annie answered quietly.

Victoria took Annie's hand in hers and together they walked into the tunnel opening. They quickly saw the bundles of earthly clothing that had been left for Jack and Dani as well as the black, two-handed sword that belonged to Belinda lying near a rough hole that had been cut by the humans upon their entry.

"Well, this is it. I can't believe this actually happened!" Jack said as he grabbed his things and went through the hole.

"If your Dad could know what you've done on this adventure he would be very proud." Dani said.

Jack smiled before breaking into a sprint and leaping over the dry creek bed that Stephen had fallen into nearly two weeks before. "Watch your step!" He called back. "Wouldn't want to fall in that in the dark!"

"Very funny Jack." Stephen grumbled as he jumped over the creek bed.

The rest of the group made their way through the forest and soon found themselves back at Belinda's farm.

"Hey, the barn lights are on." Stephen commented.

"Great Aunt Belinda must be waiting for us." Victoria said.

"Well we'd best not keep her waiting." Dani added.

The group made their way to the barn door before Annie spoke up.

"You go on ahead. I... I need a minute to myself."

"Take all the time you need Annie. When you're ready, just come inside and you can meet Aunt Belinda." Victoria said softly.

"Do you think she will like me?" Annie asked.

"I'm sure she will be thrilled to meet you." Stephen answered.

The four humans entered the barn and were greeted by Belinda who was sitting at a small table set with hot chocolate and tea. Belinda stood up from her chair and quickly rushed over to the group.

"I'm glad to see you're back safe and sound!"

"Us too." Jack added.

"I'm sure you have quite the story to tell me. But why don't you leave your things in the stalls and then we can talk the night away if you want." Belinda said.

"Aunt Belinda, there's something else we need to talk to you about." Victoria said quietly.

"Oh? And what's that?"

Annie stood outside the barn and looked up at the night sky. The stars seemed so different from the constellations she was used to. And she could hardly believe a single moon could give off so much light.

"I really am in a different world now." She mused to herself. She then heard a door open behind her and someone step out. She turned around to see a woman like her friends exit the barn. She was as tall as the twins and as stocky as Stephen. Her greyish black hair was kept in a tight bun at the nape of her neck. And to Annie's surprise, she had tears in her eyes.

"Annie?" the woman asked.

"You must be Belinda." Annie replied quietly.

Belinda slowly walked over to Annie and gave her a tight hug. "I'm so sorry you have to be here. I can understand some of what you must be going through right now. It is hard having to be away from those you love."

Annie's eyes began to water as she hugged Belinda back. "Thank you." She whispered.

"Now Steve and Tori told me all about your situation and I want you to know you are most welcome here."

"Thank you so much Belinda."

"Now why don't you come inside my house and get settled in. You can even have your own room if you want."

Annie nodded and Belinda took her hand and gently led her inside the farmhouse. Inside the barn Stephen, Tori, Dani, and Jack watched the two of them from a window.

"Looks like things are going to be ok after all." Stephen said quietly.

"Yeah. Hey Steve and Tori, thank you so much for letting us come along. It is something I will never forget." Dani said.

"It was certainly an adventure to be sure." Jack added.

"Lulandal is a beautiful place, I've been able to add a lot to my sketchbook from our journey! I wasn't able to draw everything, but I think I can add the rest from memory later." Dani said as she pulled the sketchbook from her satchel.

"I want to see those drawings!" Stephen said.

"Did you draw some of the people too?" Victoria asked.

"Why don't I show you?" Dani answered as she set her sketchbook down on the table and opened it up to a drawing of the triple moons.

And with that the group gathered around the table and started looking over Dani's drawings and talking about their adventures and the people they met.

Back at Belinda's house Annie was looking out of the window and gazing once more at the solitary moon. She sighed as she closed her eyes and fell back on the amazingly soft bed. "To the One Above, I thank you for letting me see my brother again. I ask You to keep him safe as he protects the land from the evil that has befallen it. And I ask you to please help me to be patient while I wait here until I can return. Please let Groman's battle be swift, and my return be even more so. Until then, thank you for giving me a safe place to stay with friends who care for me. I ask this in your name." She prayed silently. As she fell asleep, she wondered what adventures lay for her in this new world.

But in the back of her mind, she knew that she would one day, return to Lulandal once more.

Dani's Sketches.

To my friend The Author.

Here are the sketches you requested from the ones I made while on my adventure in Lulandal. I've gone over them a bit like you asked and made sure they were satisfactory. I hope these are what you wanted. I look forward to reading futures stories from our friends in Lulandal.

Best Regards.

Danielle Briggs-Wyng.

Monaria

Can sometimes see the future
10 in. Tall
wears Clothes made from flowers & tree bark

Peregrine

Excellent flier
Razor sharp talons on hands and feet.
feathers look like a peregrine falcon
very fiesty

Annie

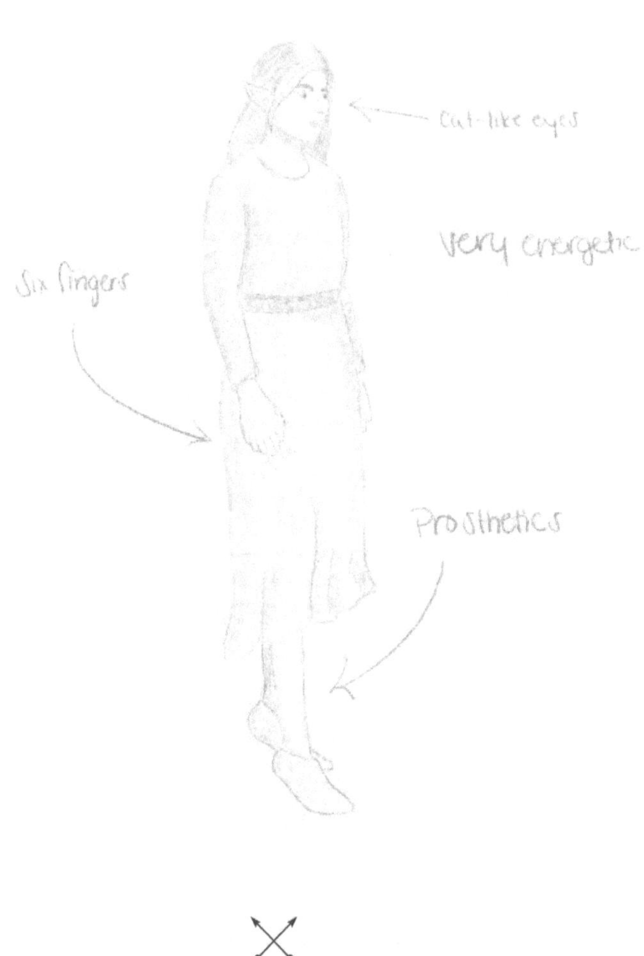

Tiny
REALLY Sharp Teeth
10 ft tall
looks mean, but really a big teddy bear

Saralia

About the Author

Hi there! I'm Jonathan Zobel, the author of this book. I'm a big history nut and I grew up reading many many books throughout my childhood and teen years and I've always enjoyed a good story. I was homeschooled by my parent's all the way through high shcool and I attended Faith Baptist Bible college in Ankeny IA for two years, graduating with an AA. I was a playwright for a few years before I shifted to writing books.